EEK & ACK VS THE WOLFMAN

STONE ARCH BOOKS
stonearchbooks.com

Graphic Sparks are published by Stone Arch Books,
A Capstone Imprint
151 Good Counsel Drive, P.O. Box 669
Mankato, Minnesota 56002
www.capstonepub.com

Library of Congress Cataloging-in-Publication Data
Hoena, B. A.
Eek and Ack vs the Wolfman / by Blake A. Hoena; illustrated by Steve Harpster.
p. cm. — (Graphic Sparks. Eek and Ack)
ISBN 978-1-4342-1189-7 (library binding)
ISBN 978-1-4342-1389-1 (pbk.)
1. Graphic novels. [1. Graphic novels. 2. Extraterrestrial beings—Fiction.
3. Halloween—Fiction.] I. Harpster, Steve, ill. II. Title.
PZ7.7.H64Eek 2009
[Fic]—dc22
2008032057

Summary: What's the best day for an alien invasion? Halloween, of course. When Eek
and Ack visit Earth during the ghoulish holiday, they fit right in with the other trick-or-
treaters. Unfortunately, so does Wolfy the Wolfman! Now, the terrible twosome must fight
off this frightful furball or fail to conquer Earth once again.

Creative Director: Heather Kindseth
Graphic Designer: Emily Harris

Printed in the United States of America in Stevens Point, Wisconsin.
052010
005814R

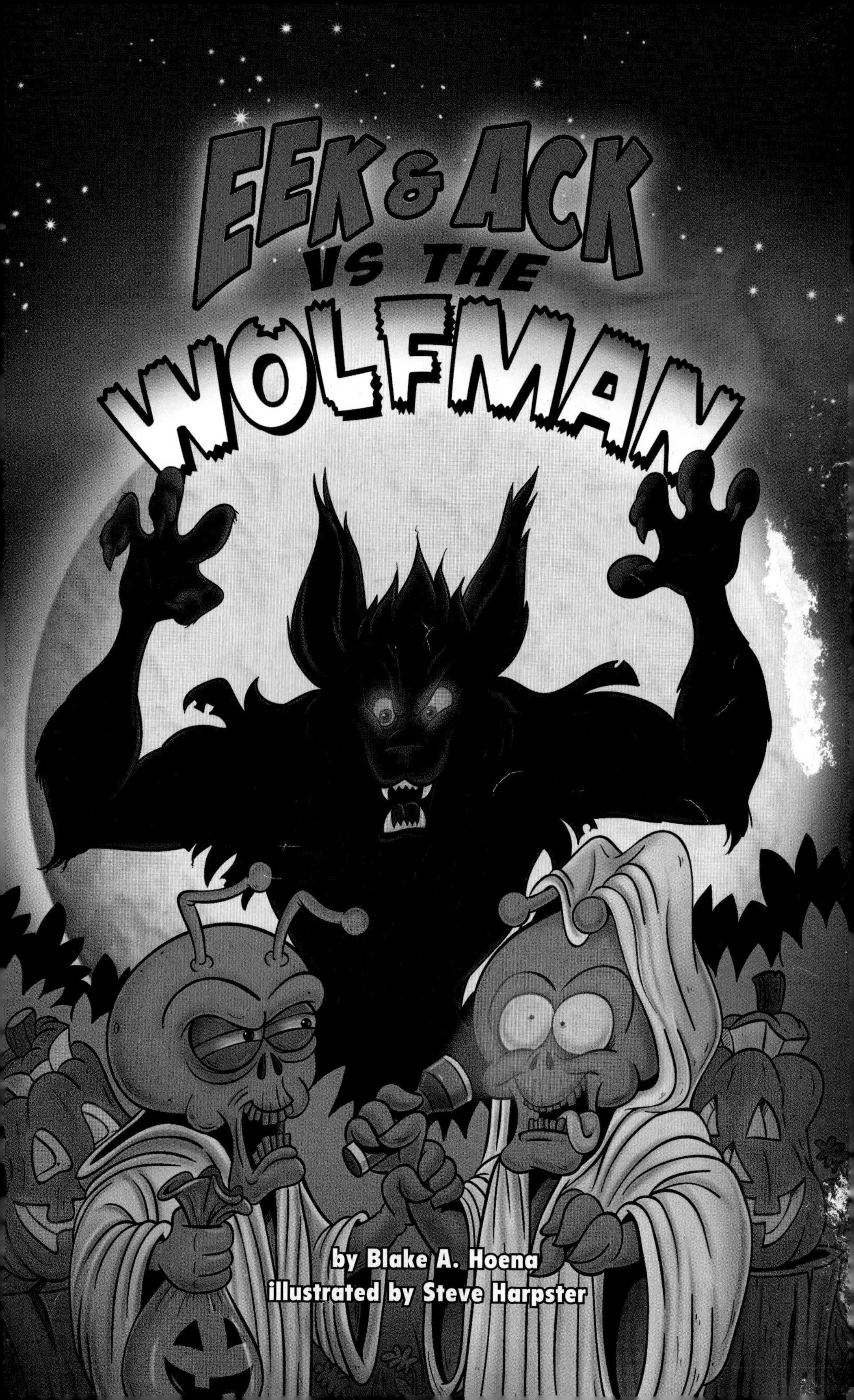
EEK & ACK
VS THE
WOLFMAN
by Blake A. Hoena
illustrated by Steve Harpster

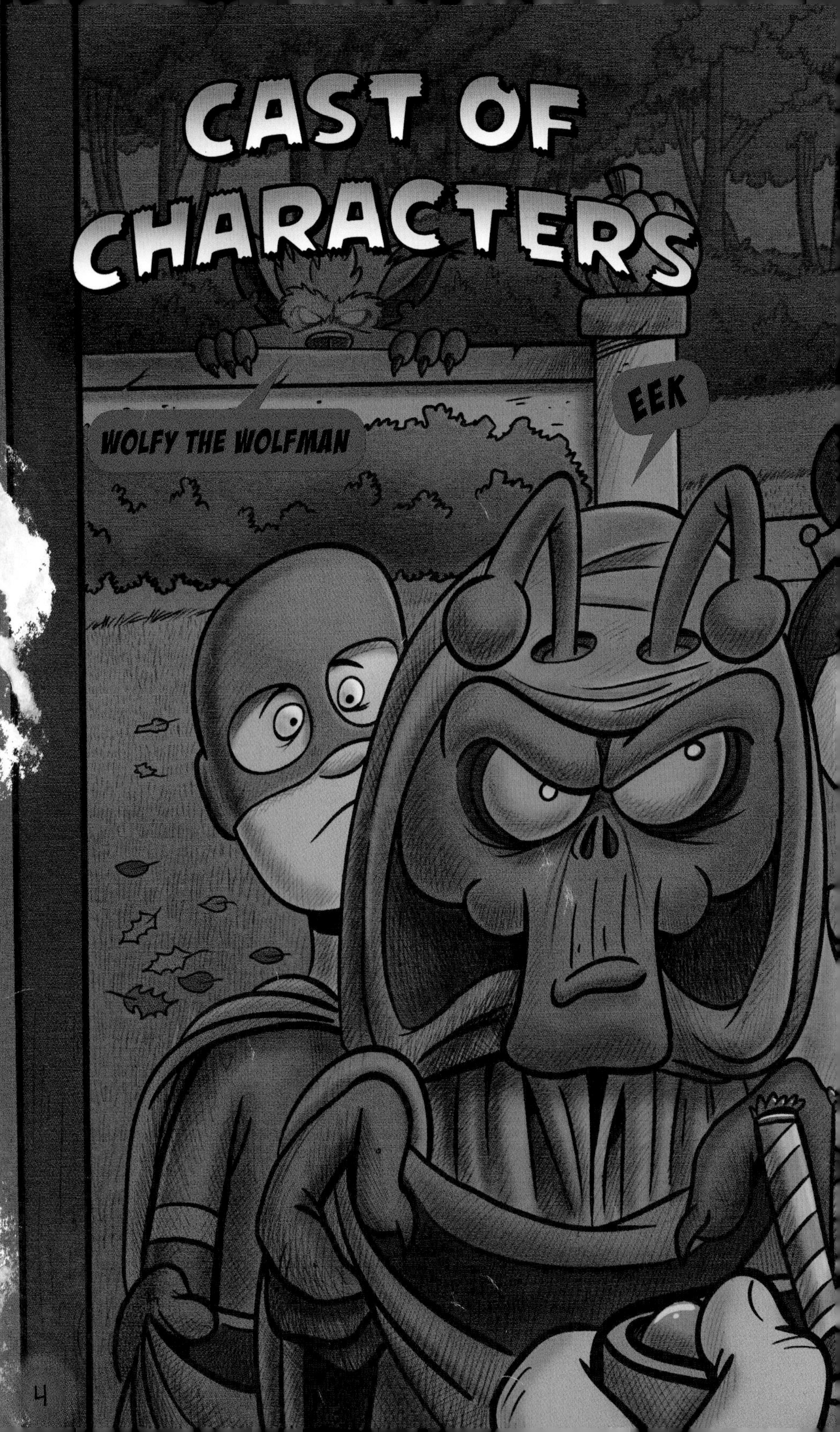
CAST OF CHARACTERS
WOLFY THE WOLFMAN
EEK

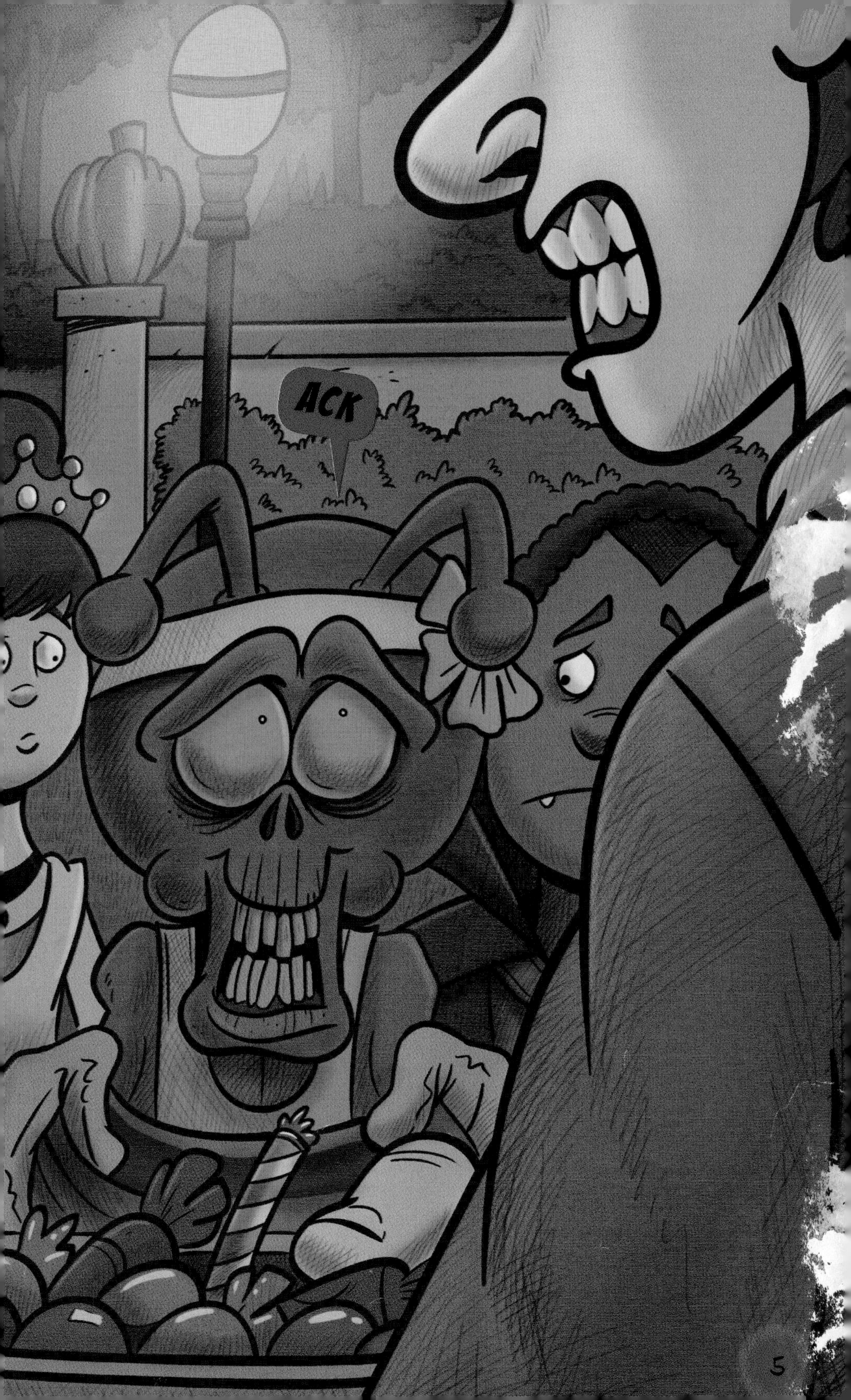
ACK

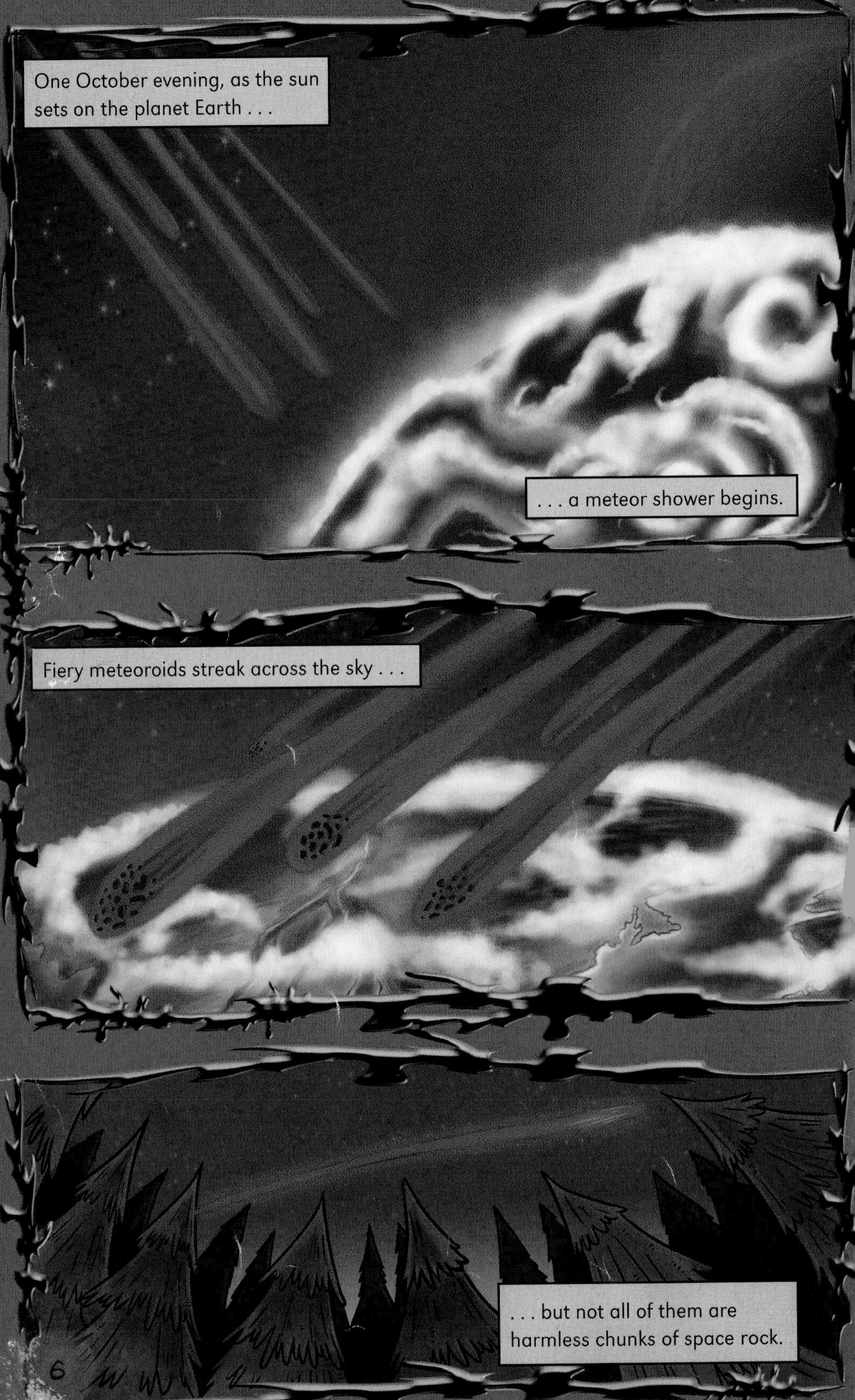
One October evening, as the sun sets on the planet Earth . . .
. . . a meteor shower begins.
Fiery meteoroids streak across the sky . . .
. . . but not all of them are harmless chunks of space rock.

Our favorite space aliens, Eek and Ack, are using the meteor shower to hide their approach to Earth.

Ha! This is my sneakiest sinister plot yet.
But, Eek, there's one thing I don't get.

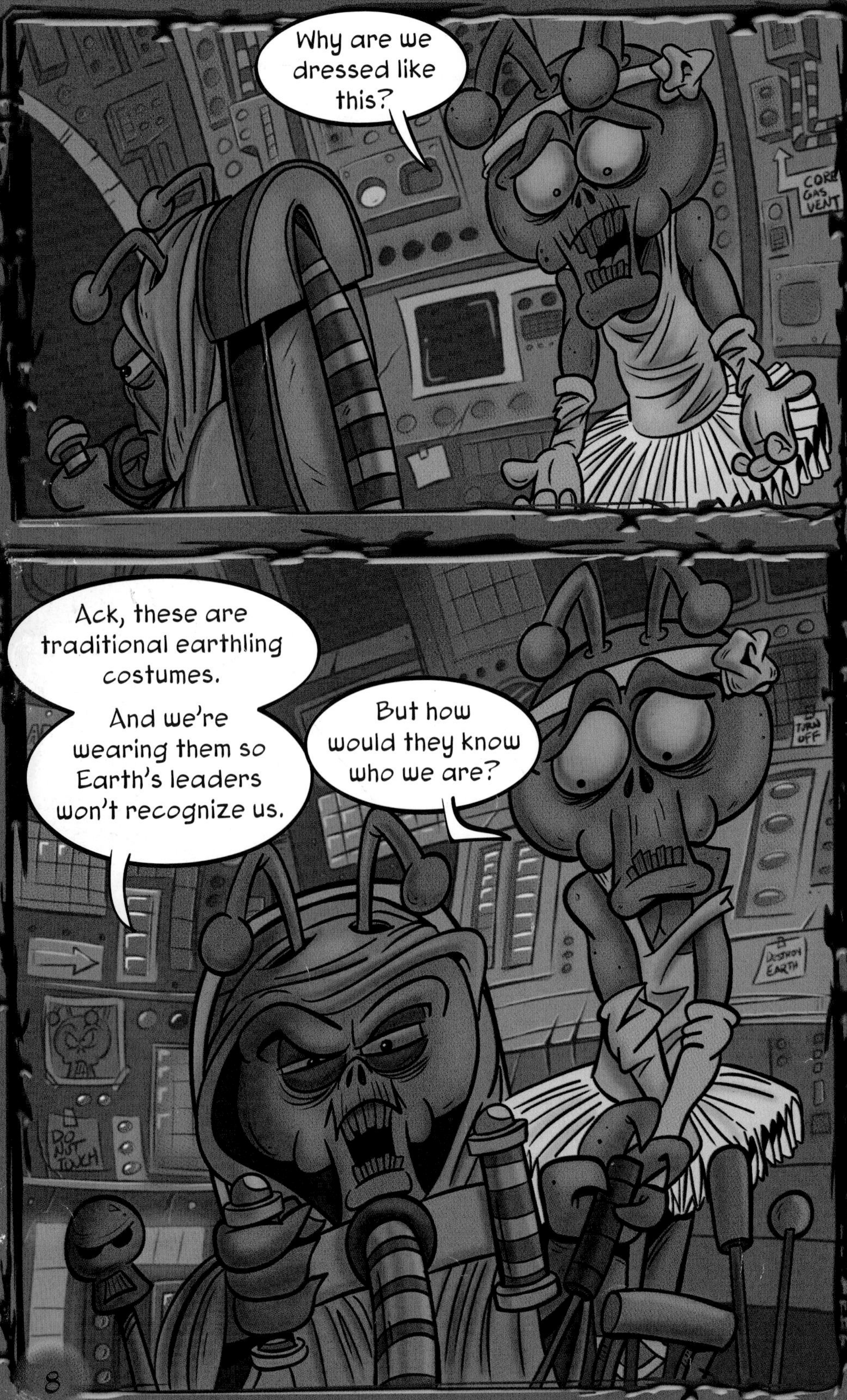
Why are we dressed like this?
CORE GAS VENT
Ack, these are traditional earthling costumes.
And we're wearing them so Earth's leaders won't recognize us.
But how would they know who we are?
TURN OFF
DESTROY EARTH
DO NOT TOUCH

Remember what happened to Uncle Icky when he crashed near that Roswell place?
An earthling took a picture of him, so Earth's leaders must know what he looks like.
And Mom always says you look like Icky.
Do not! I've got all my teeth. See!

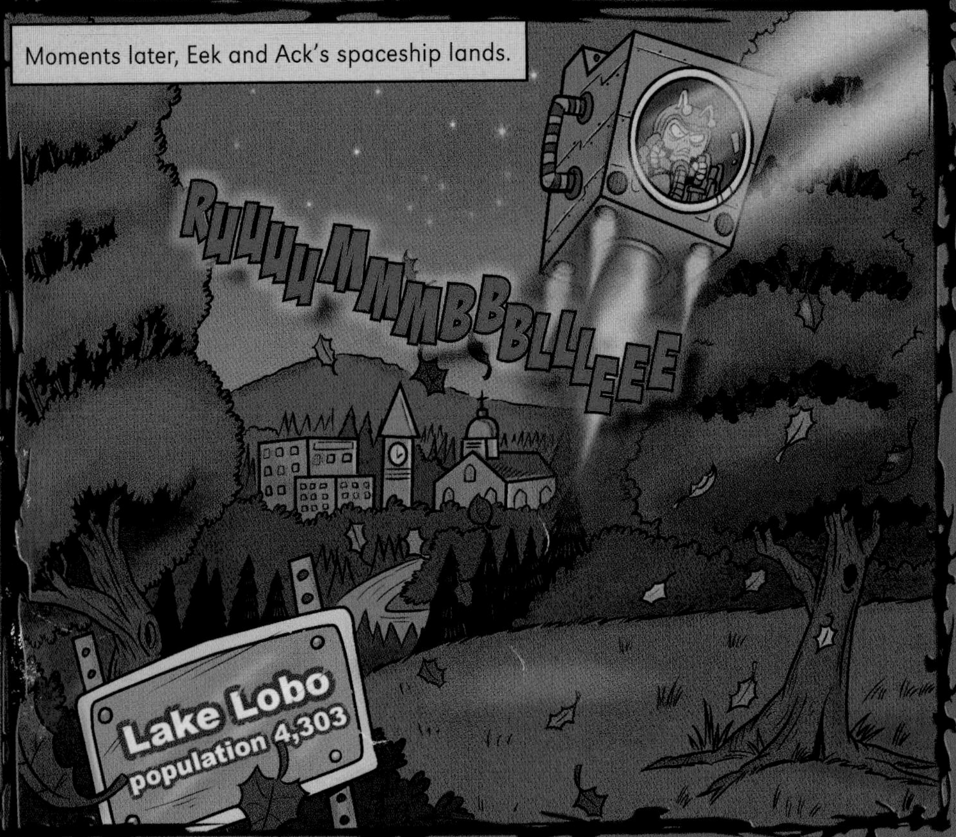
Moments later, Eek and Ack's spaceship lands.
RUUUUMMMBBBLLLEEE
Lake Lobo
population 4,303

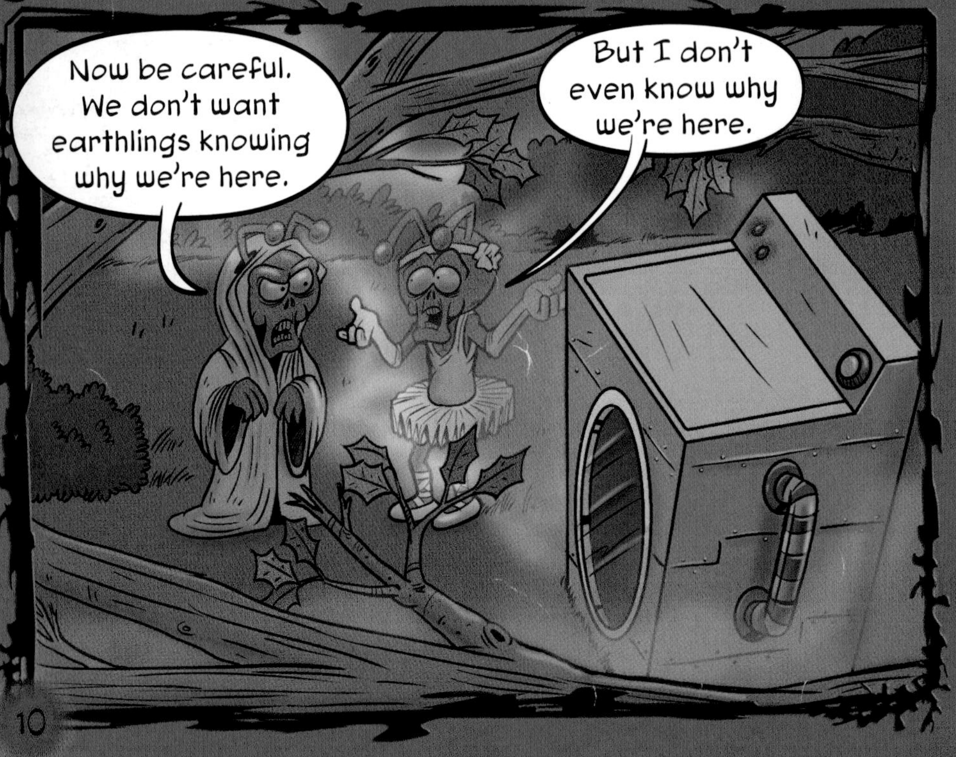
Now be careful. We don't want earthlings knowing why we're here.
But I don't even know why we're here.

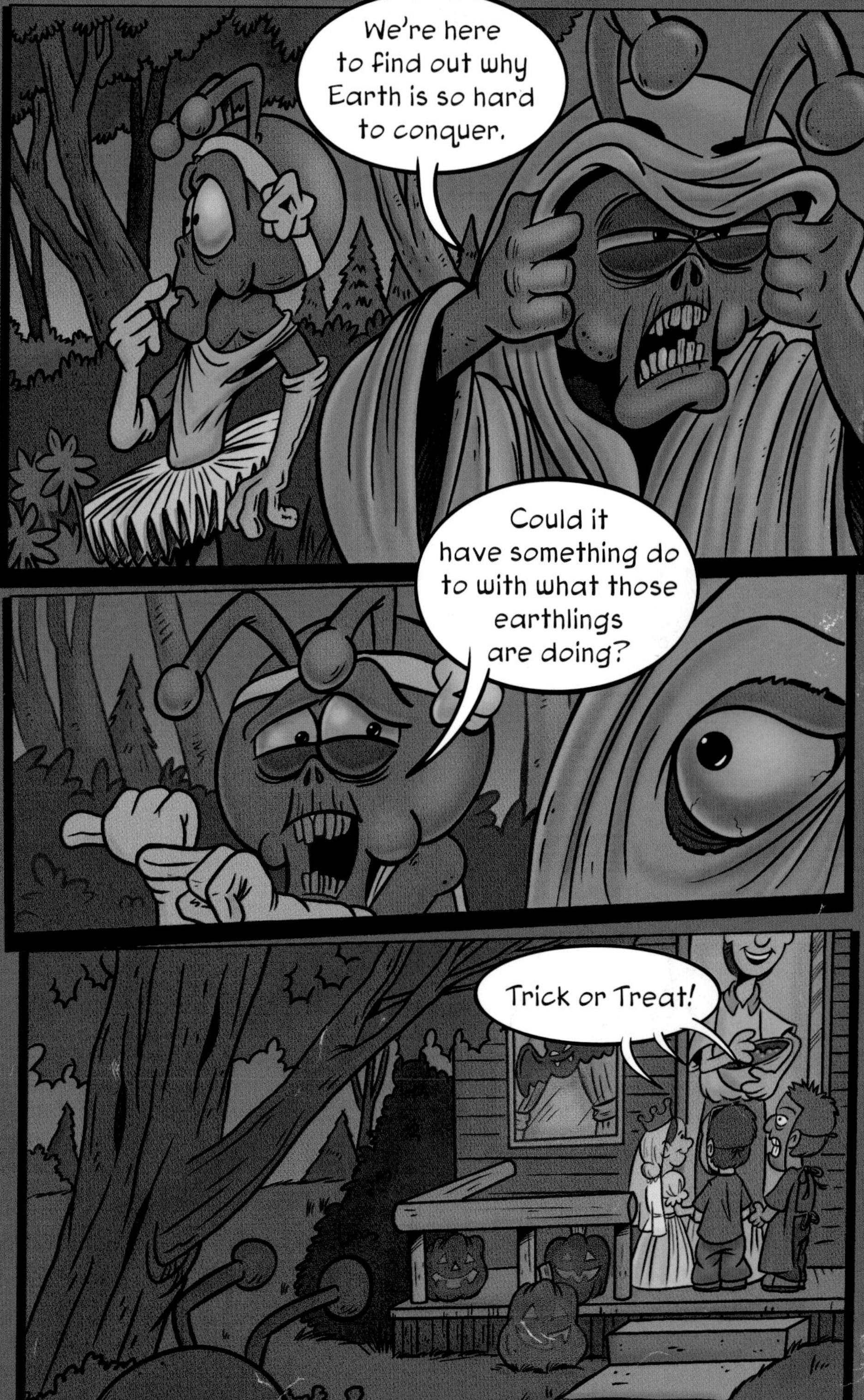
We're here to find out why Earth is so hard to conquer.
Could it have something do to with what those earthlings are doing?
Trick or Treat!

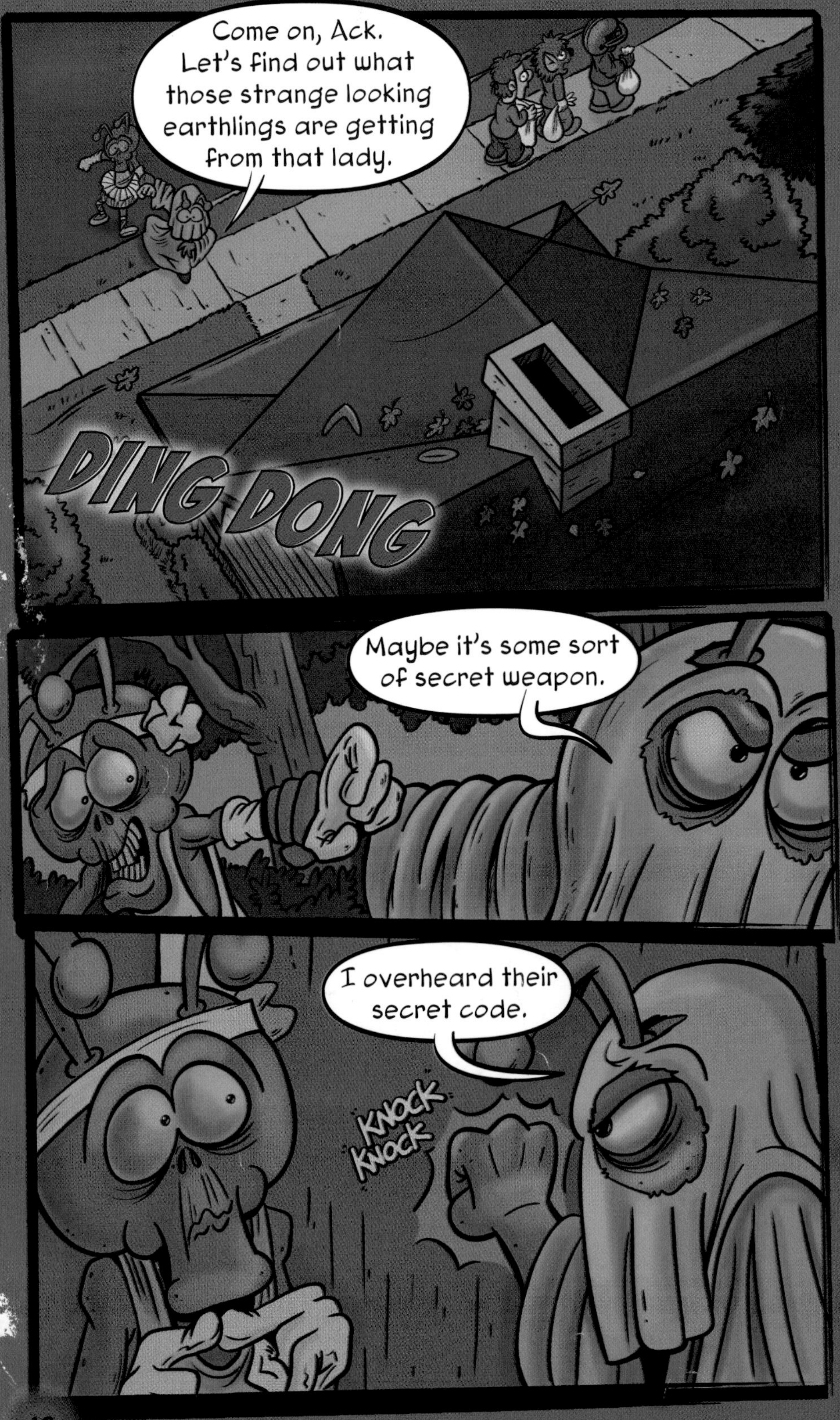
Come on, Ack. Let's find out what those strange looking earthlings are getting from that lady.
DING DONG
Maybe it's some sort of secret weapon.
I overheard their secret code.
KNOCK KNOCK

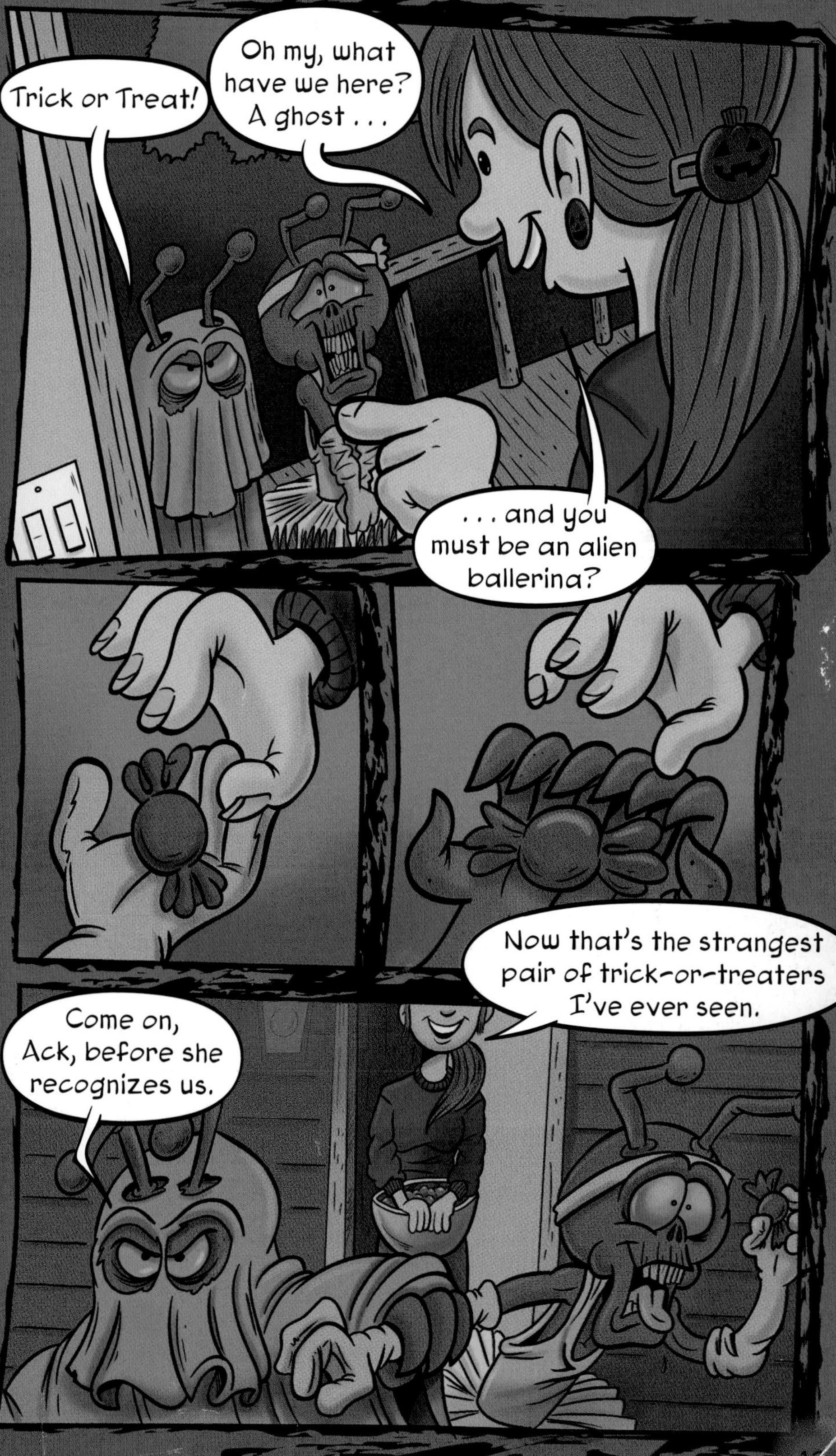
Trick or Treat!
Oh my, what have we here? A ghost . . .
. . . and you must be an alien ballerina?
Now that's the strangest pair of trick-or-treaters I've ever seen.
Come on, Ack, before she recognizes us.

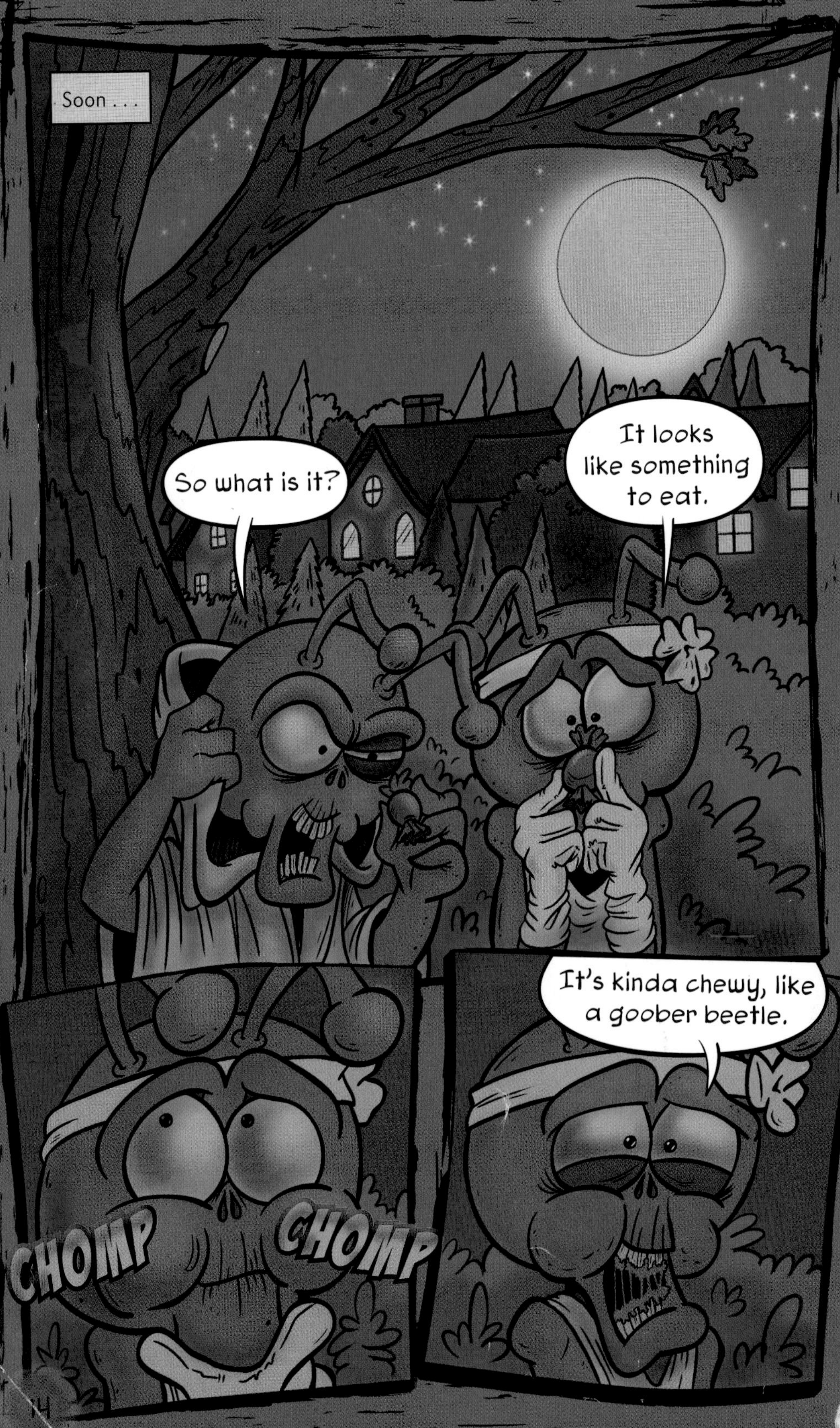
Soon . . .
So what is it?
It looks like something to eat.
CHOMP
CHOMP
It's kinda chewy, like a goober beetle.

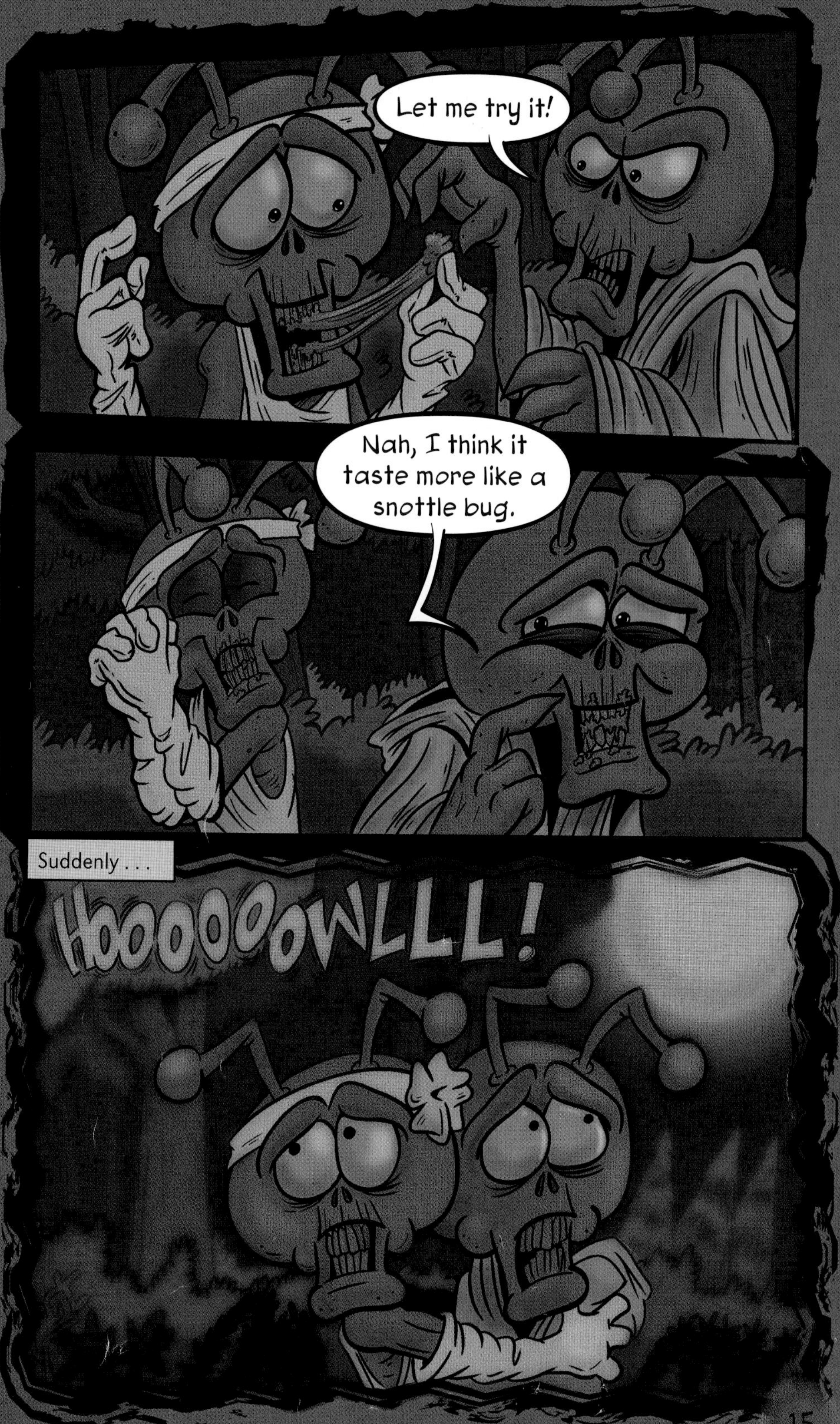

Let me try it!
Nah, I think it taste more like a snottle bug.
Suddenly . . .
HOOOOOOWLLL!

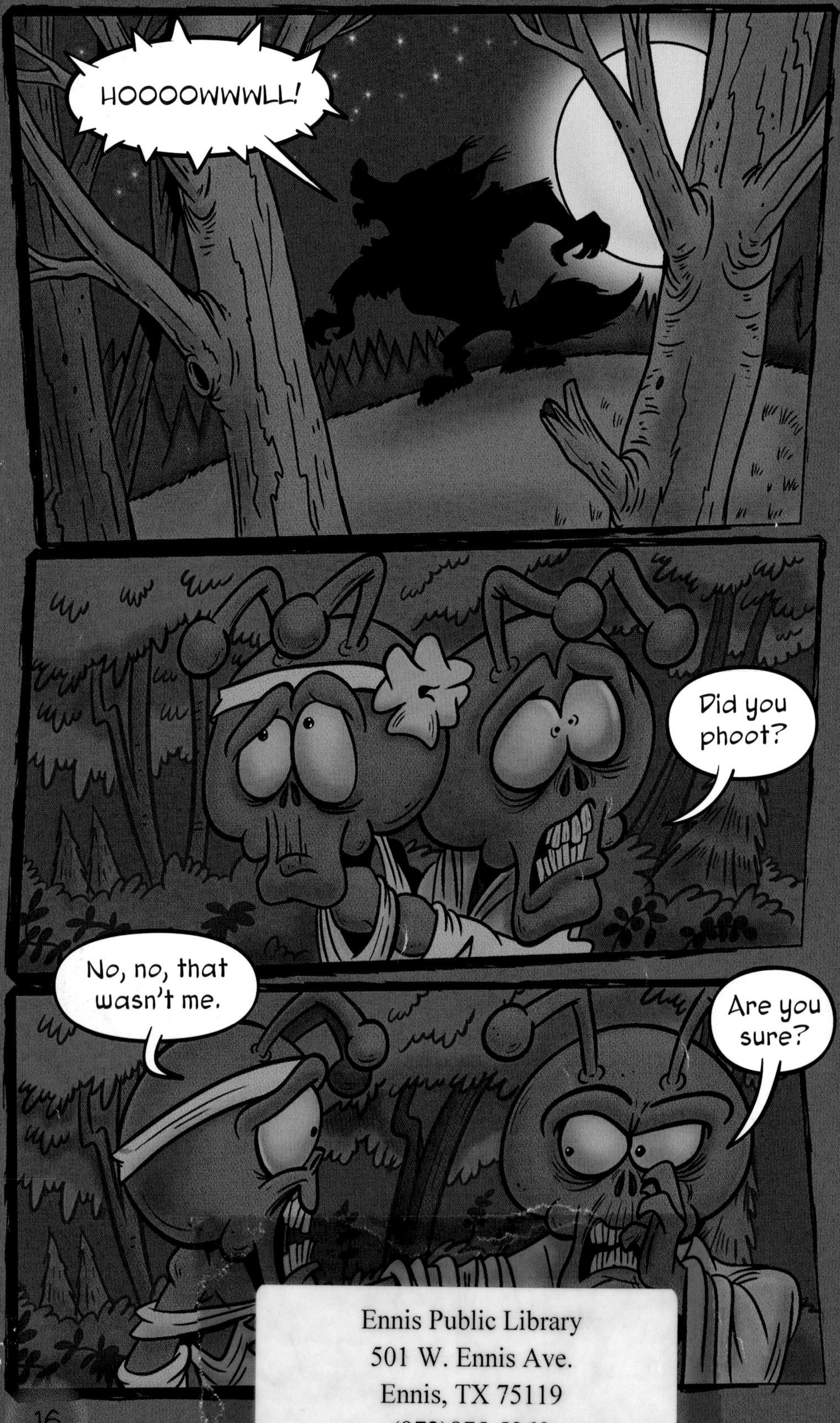
HOOOOWWWLL!
Did you phoot?
No, no, that wasn't me.
Are you sure?

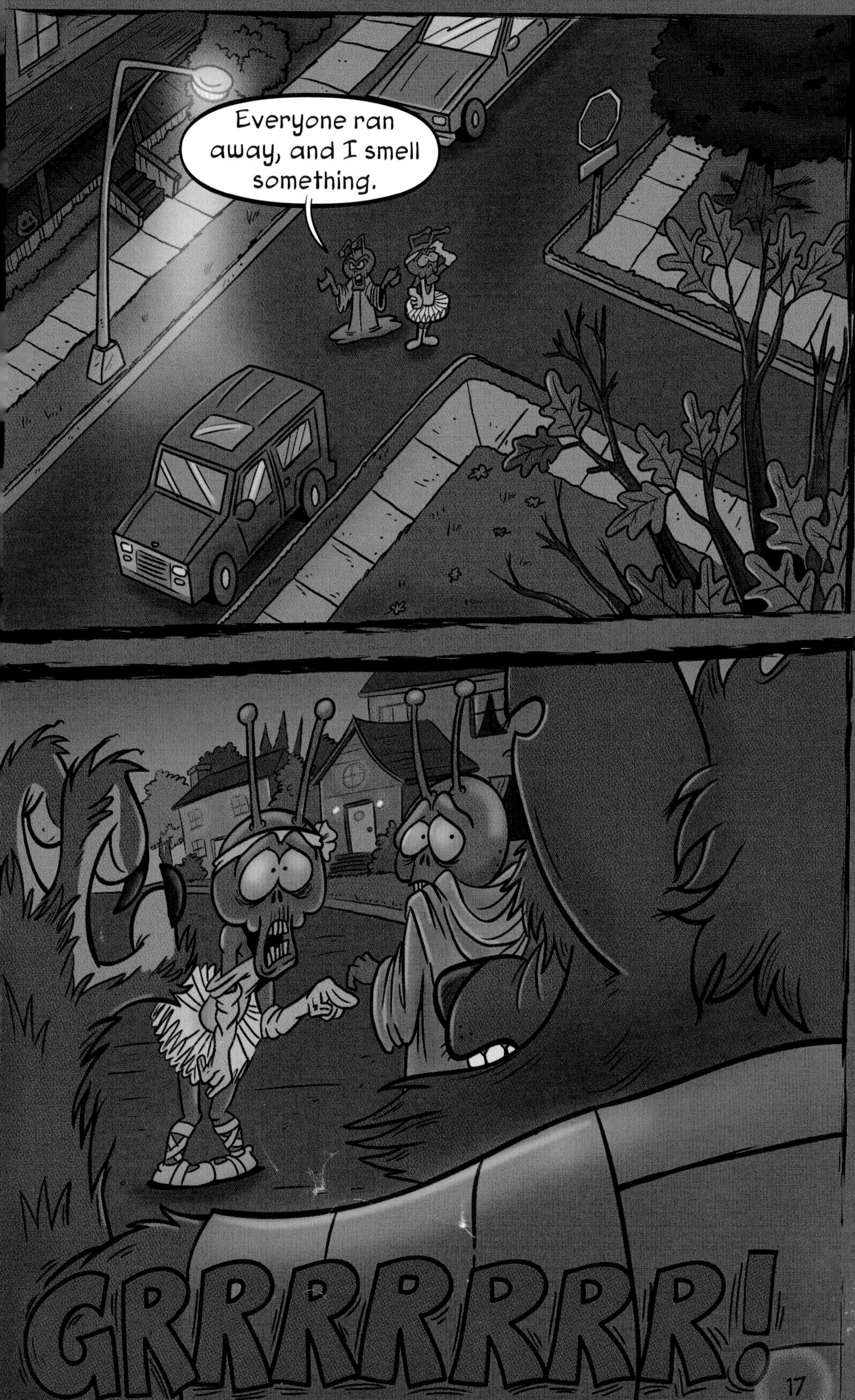
Everyone ran away, and I smell something.
GRRRRRRR!

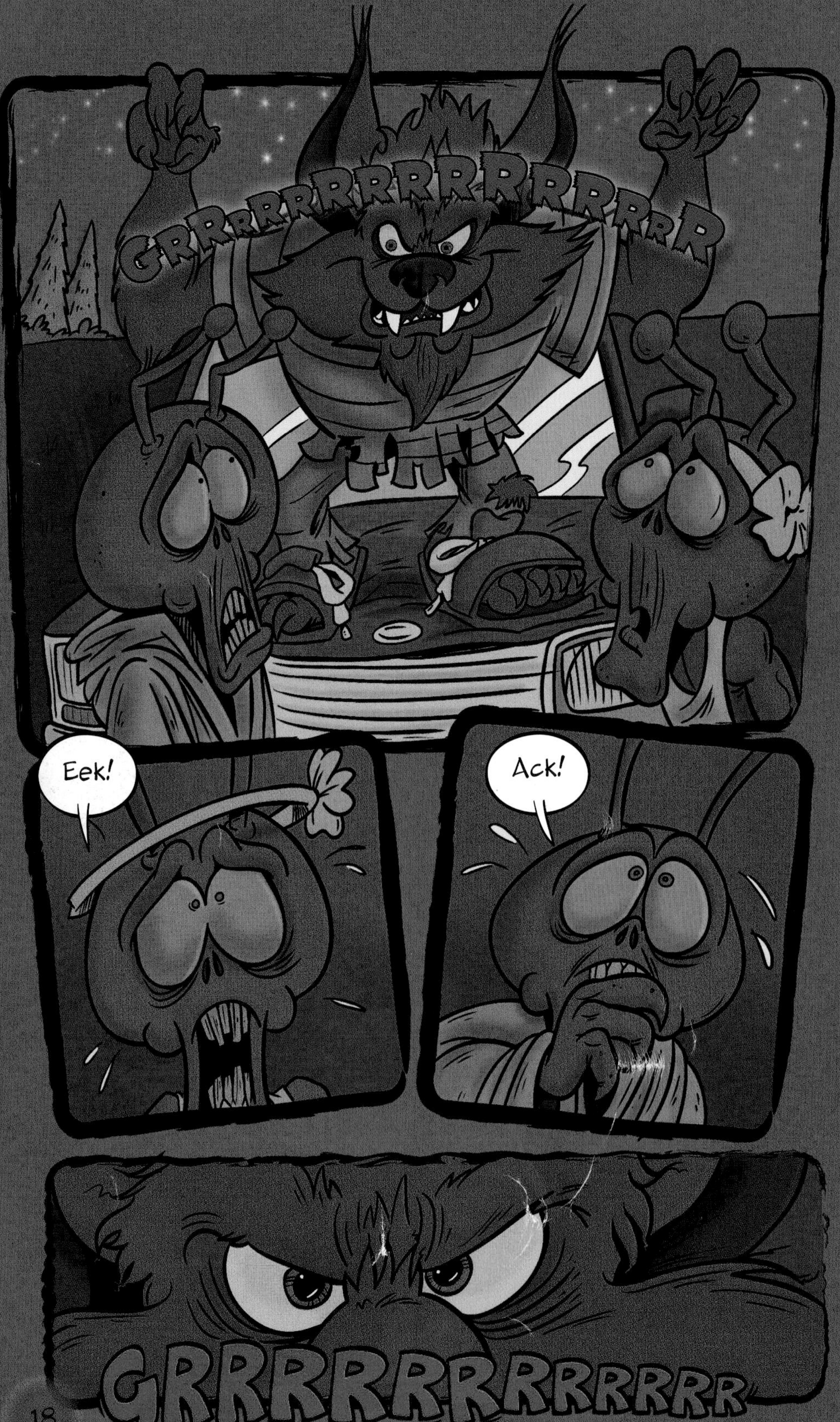
GRRRRRRRRRRRRRRR
Eek!
Ack!
GRRRRRRRRRRRR

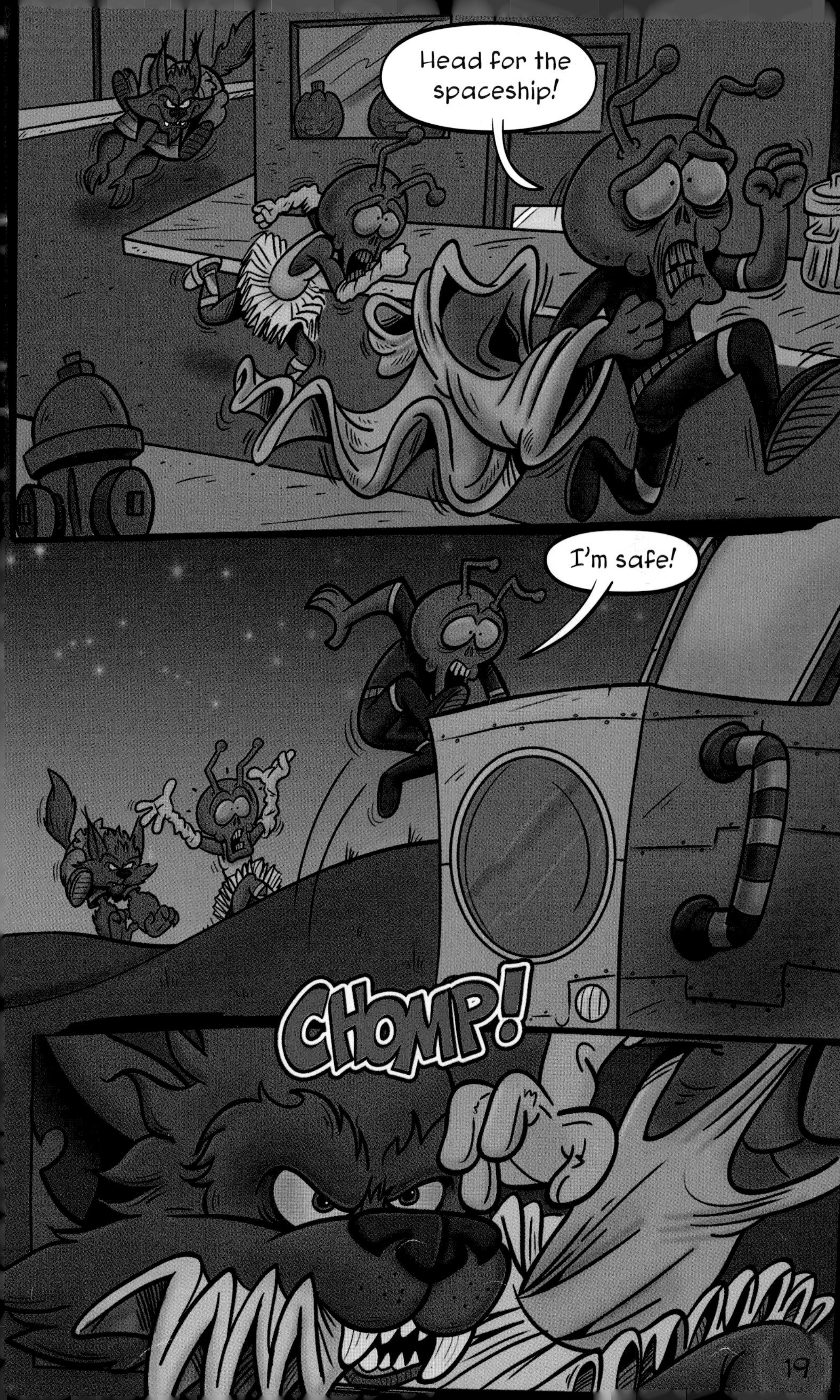

Head for the spaceship!
I'm safe!
CHOMP!

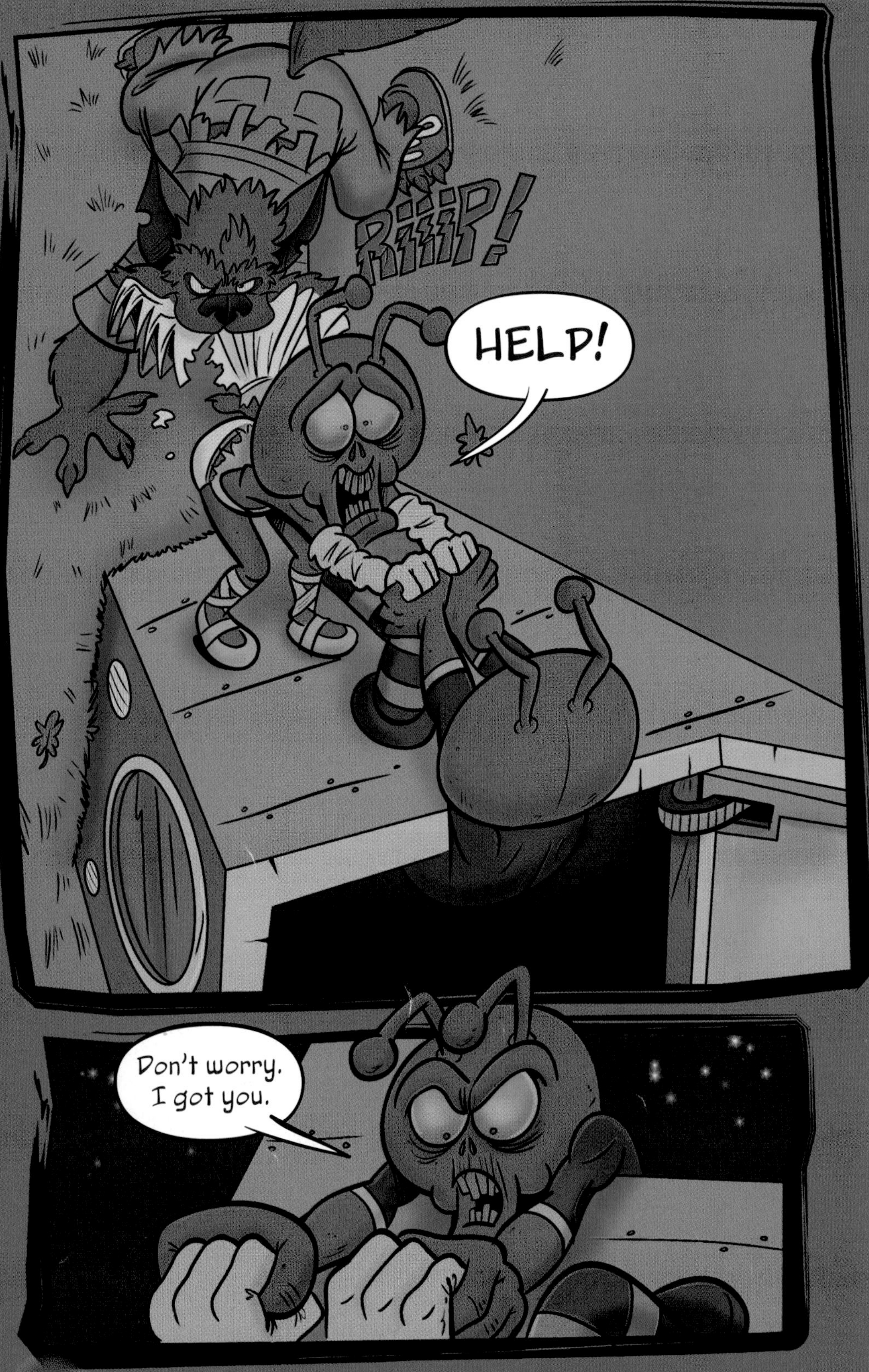
RIIIIP!
HELP!
Don't worry. I got you.

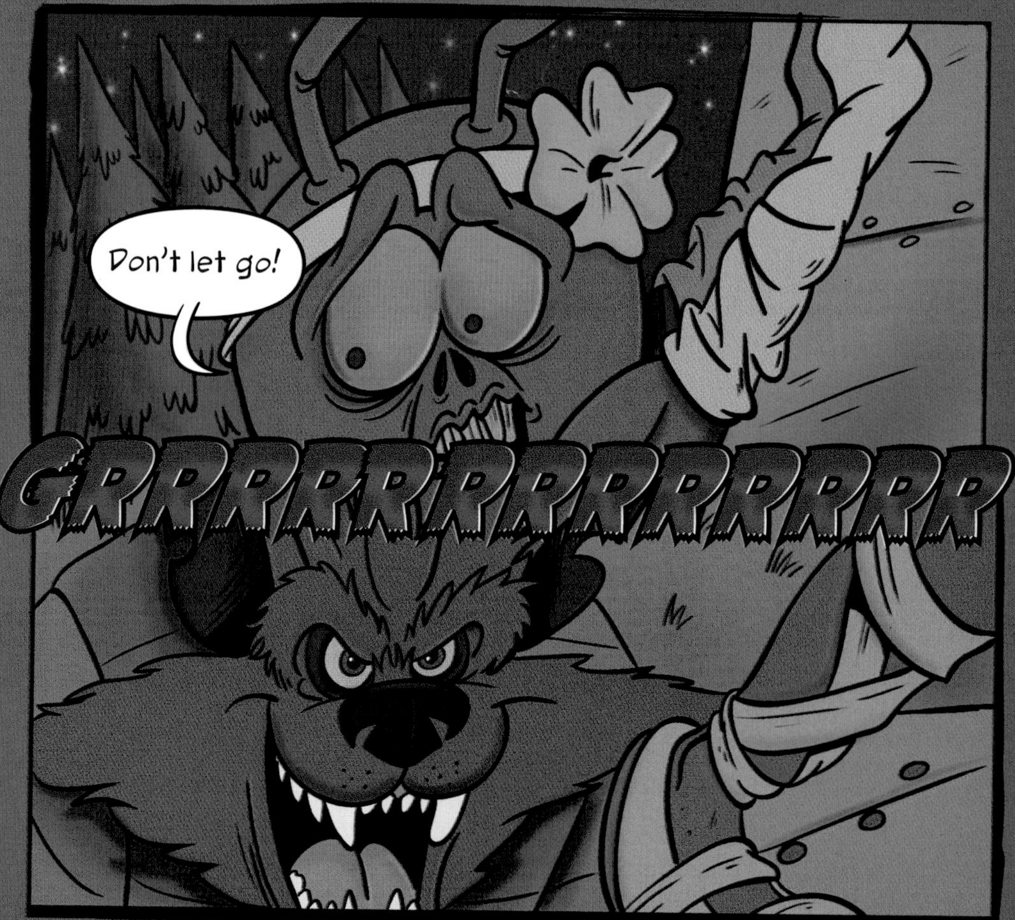
Don't let go!
GRRRRRRRRRRRRRRR

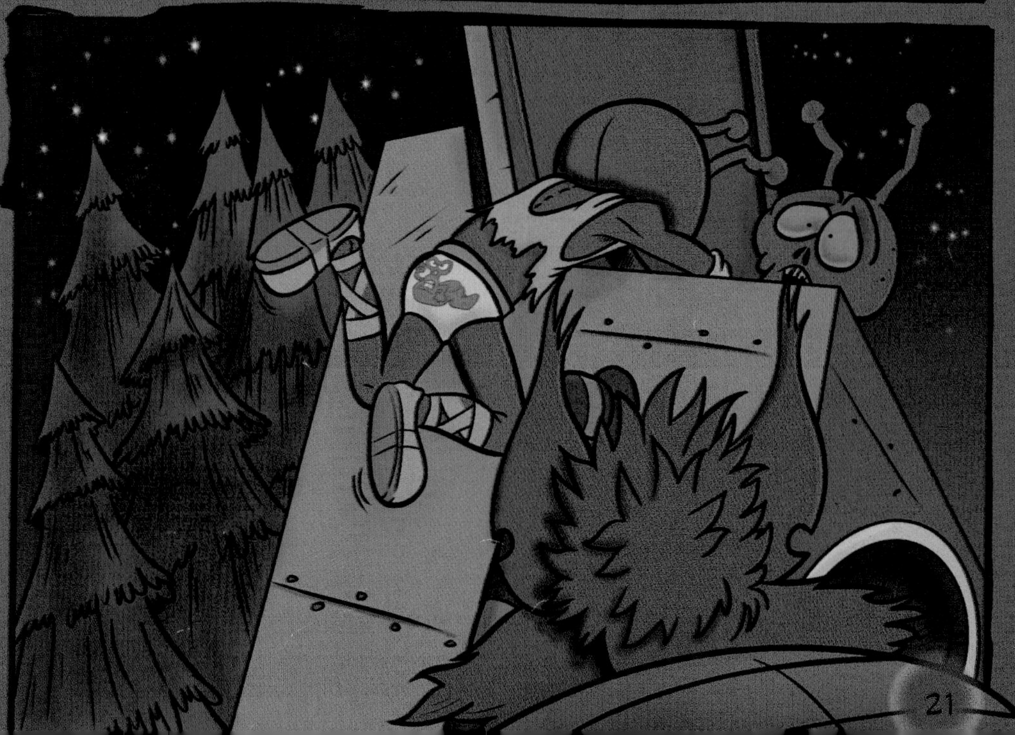

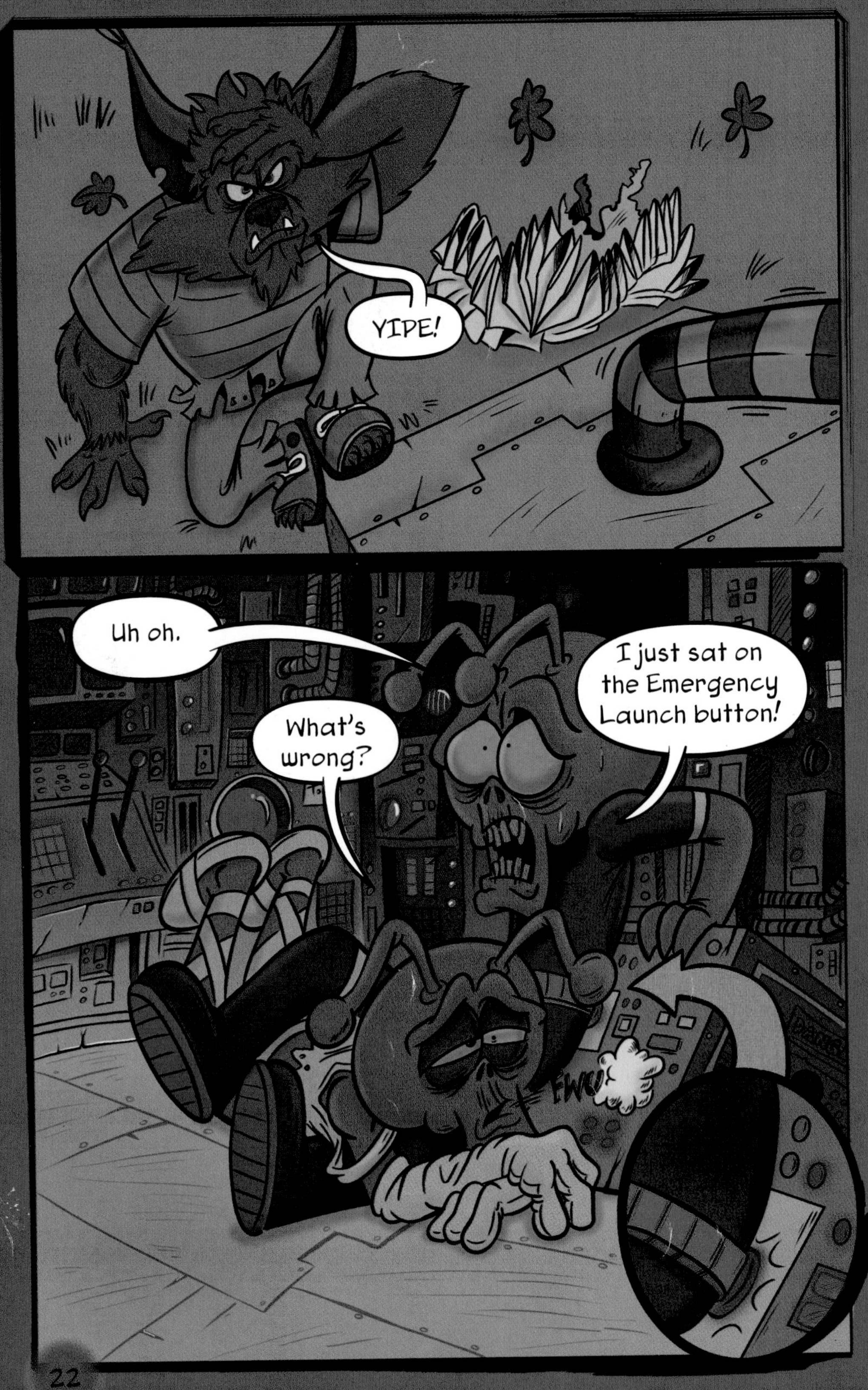
YIPE!
Uh oh.
What's wrong?
I just sat on the Emergency Launch button!
FWU

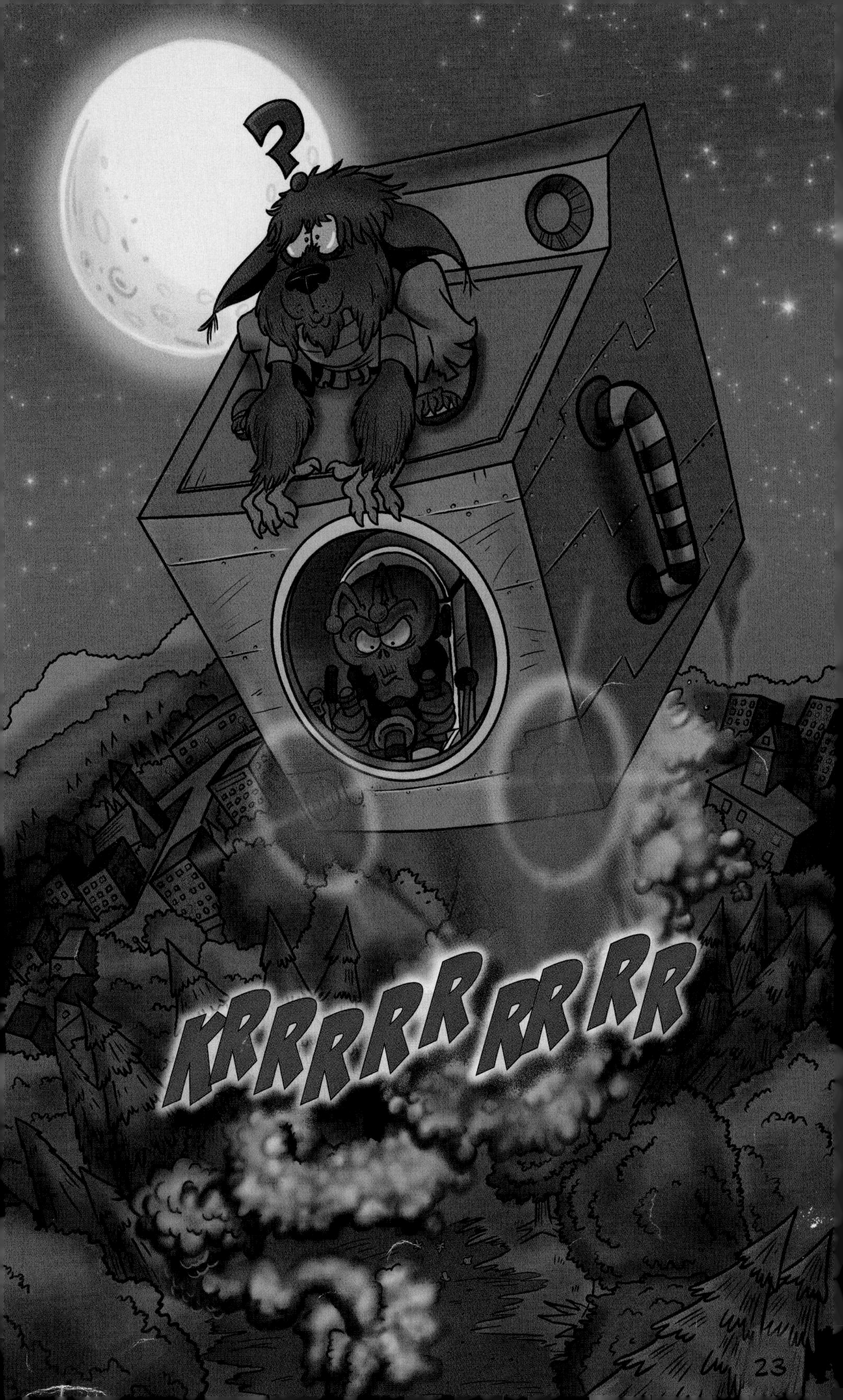
?
KRRRRR RR RR

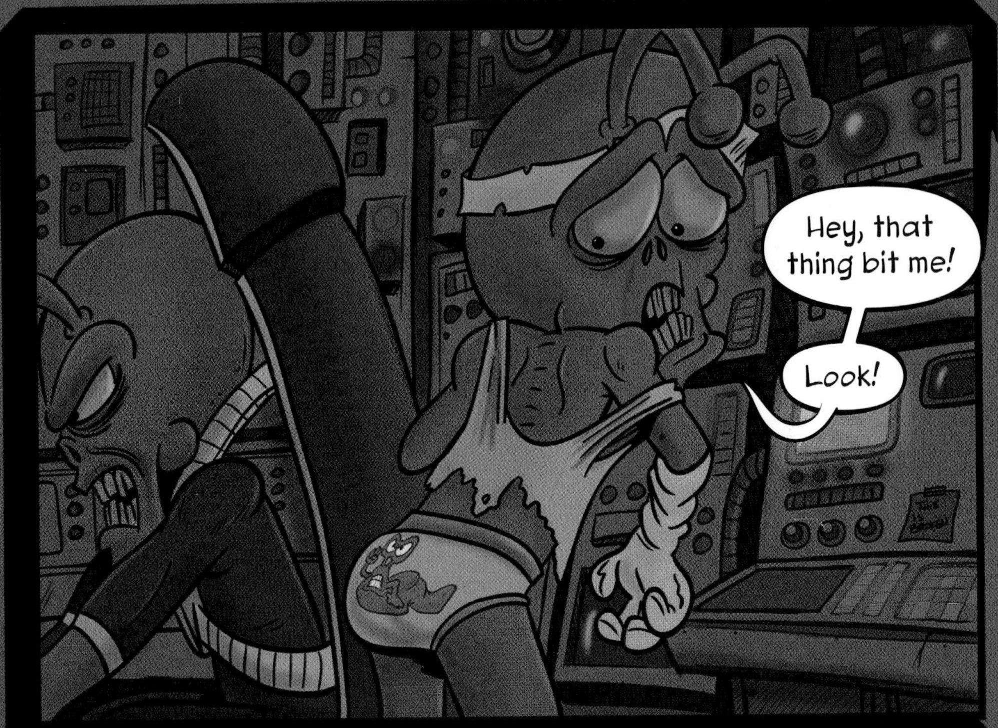
Hey, that thing bit me!
Look!

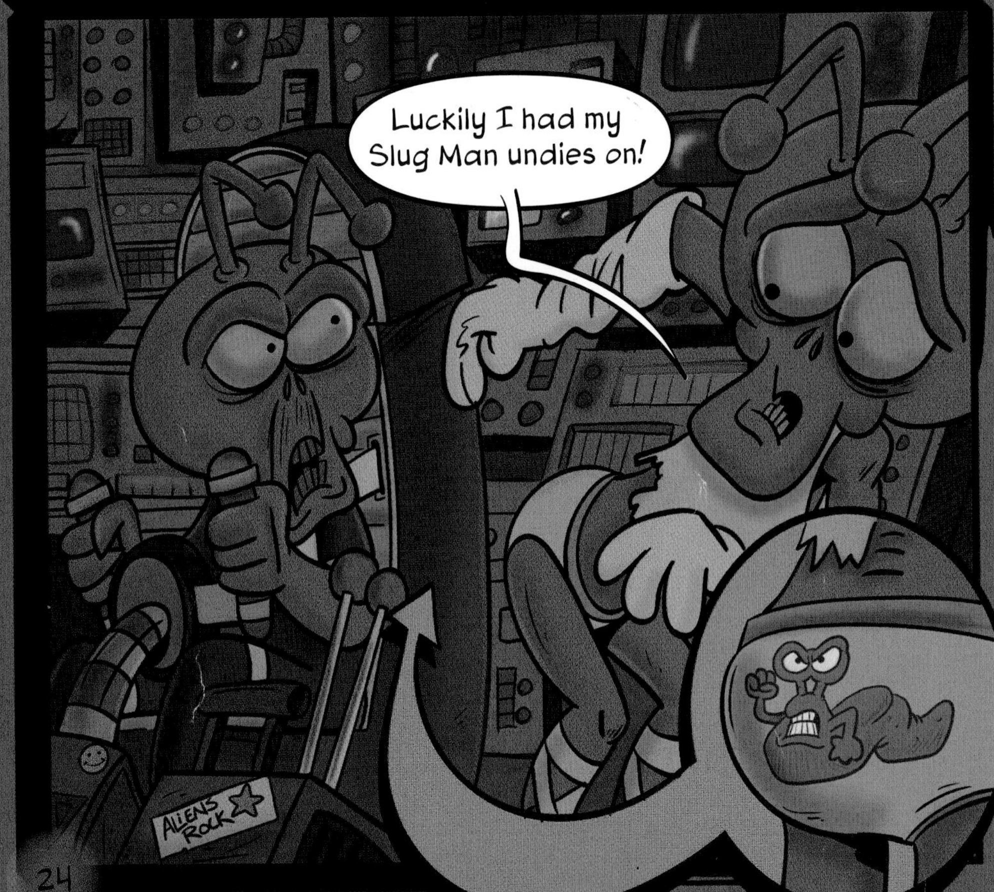
Luckily I had my Slug Man undies on!
ALIENS ROCK

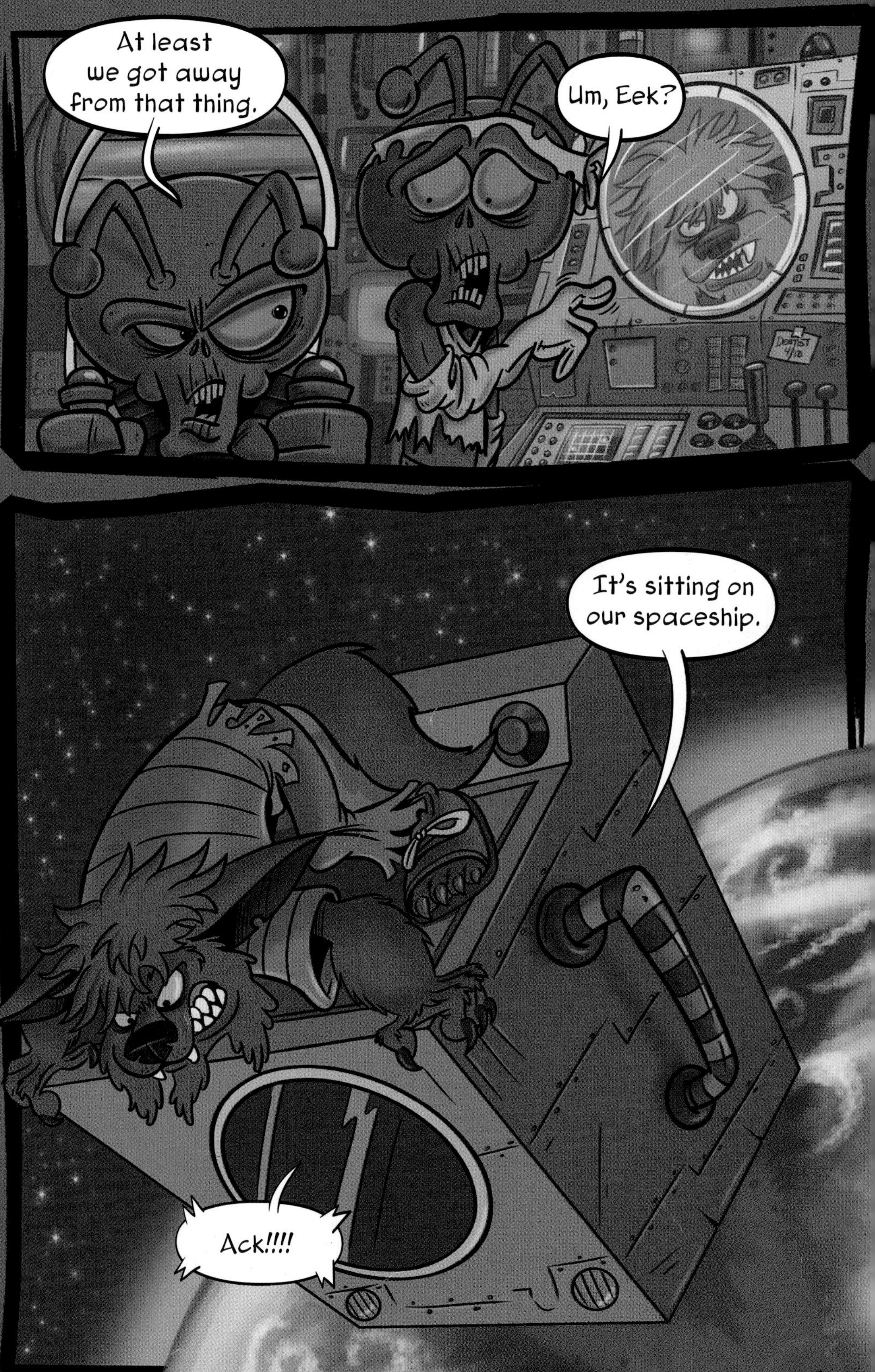
At least we got away from that thing.
Um, Eek?
It's sitting on our spaceship.
Ack!!!!

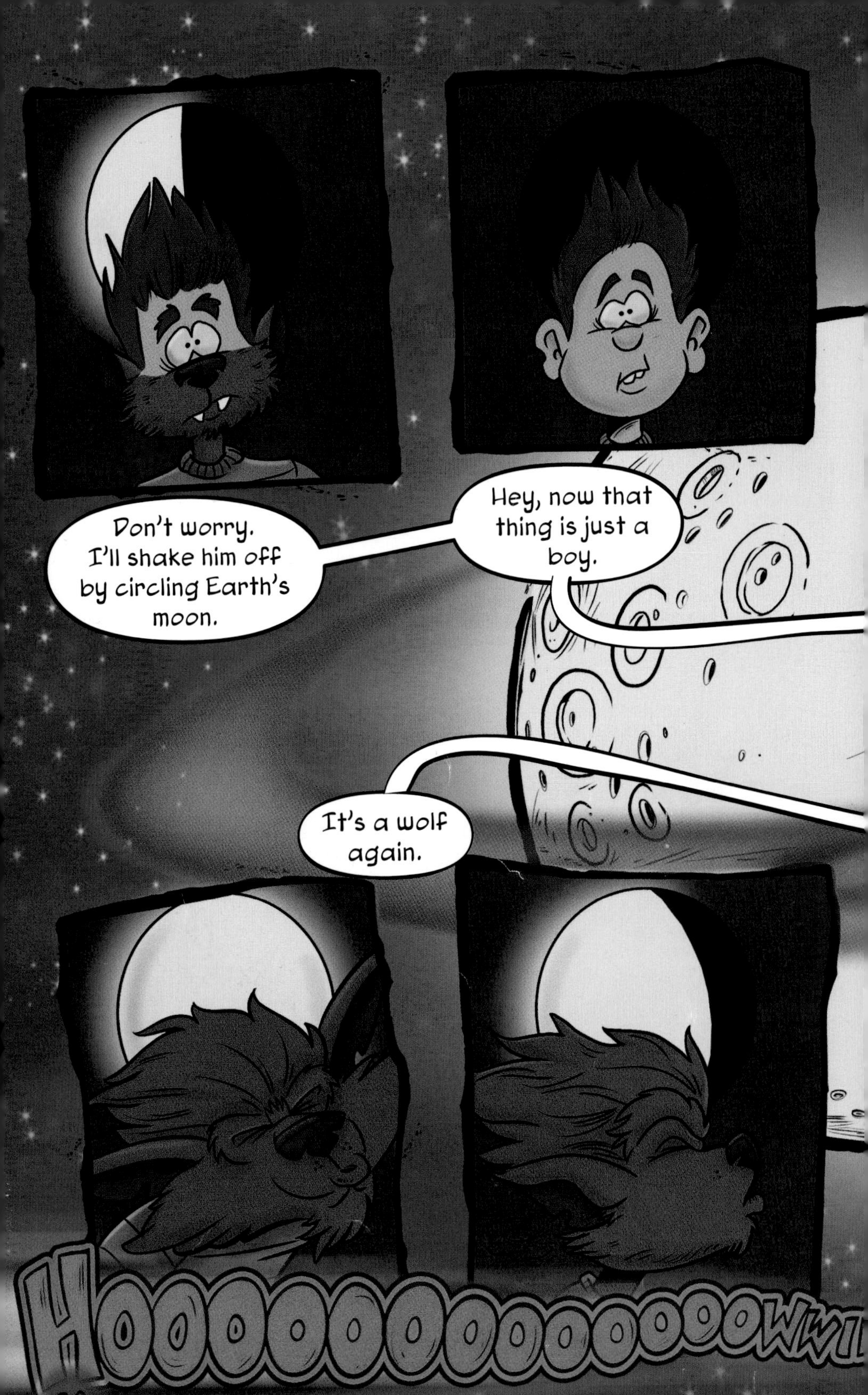
Don't worry. I'll shake him off by circling Earth's moon.
Hey, now that thing is just a boy.
It's a wolf again.
HOOOOOOOOOOOOOOWWL

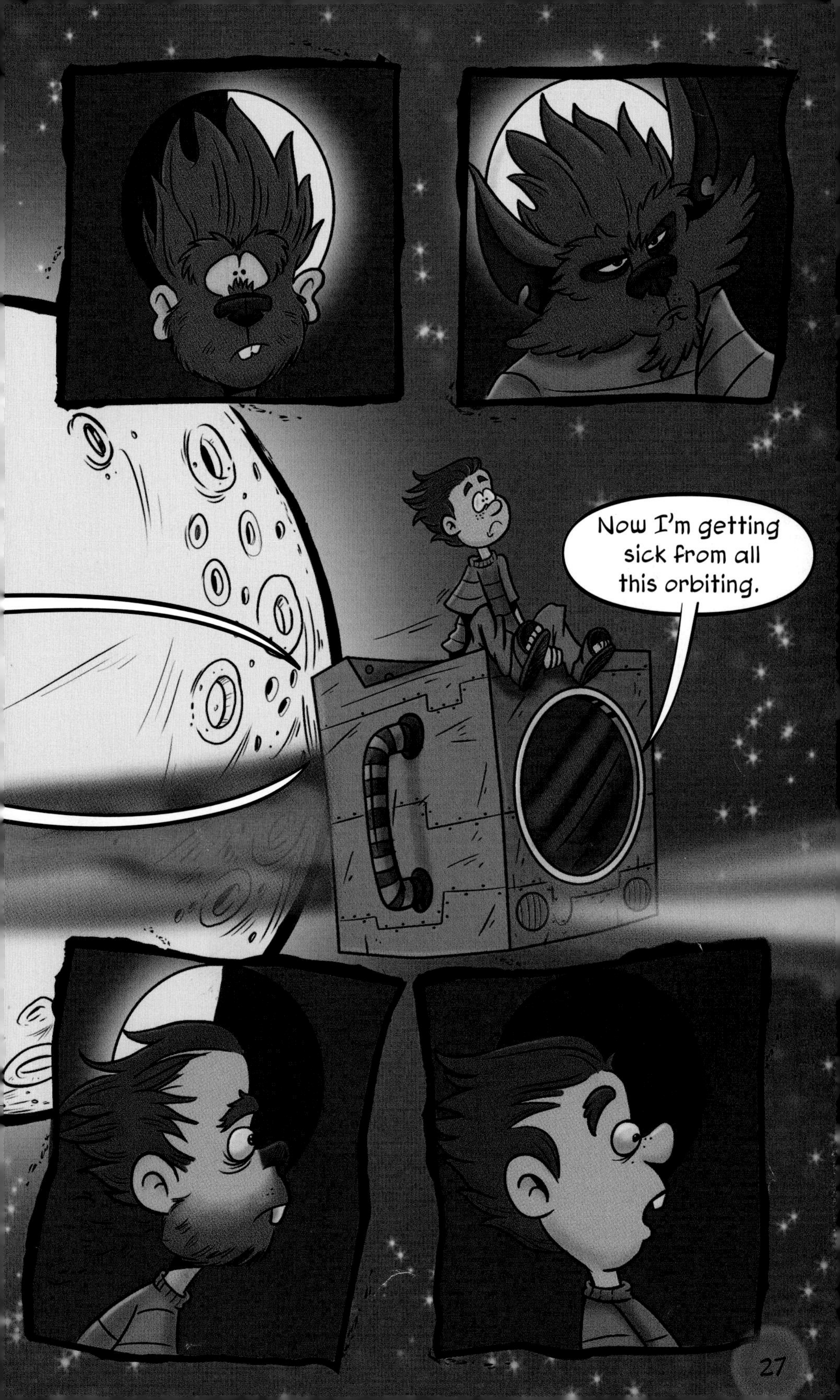
Now I'm getting sick from all this orbiting.

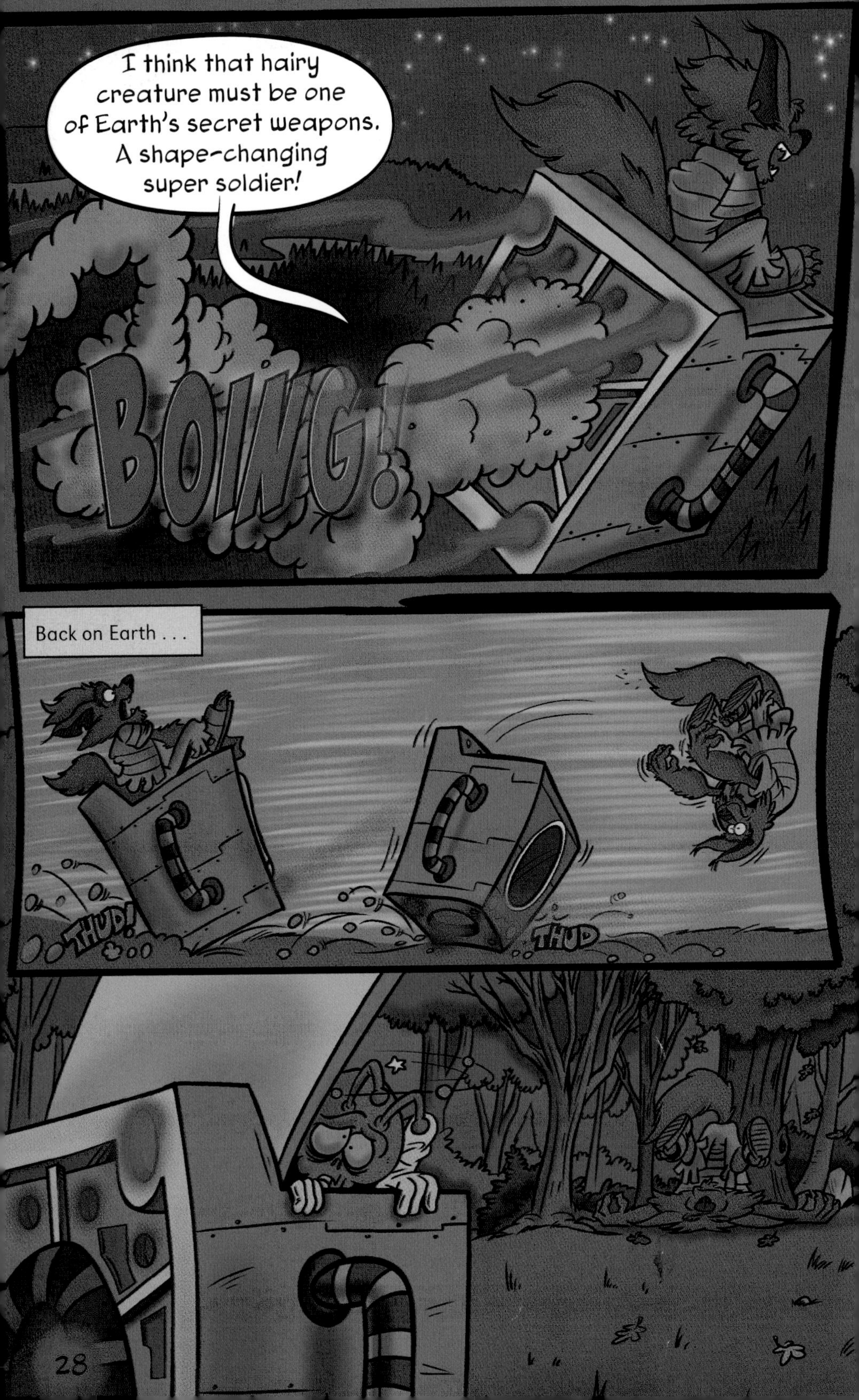

I think that hairy creature must be one of Earth's secret weapons. A shape-changing super soldier!
BOING!
Back on Earth . . .
THUD!
THUD

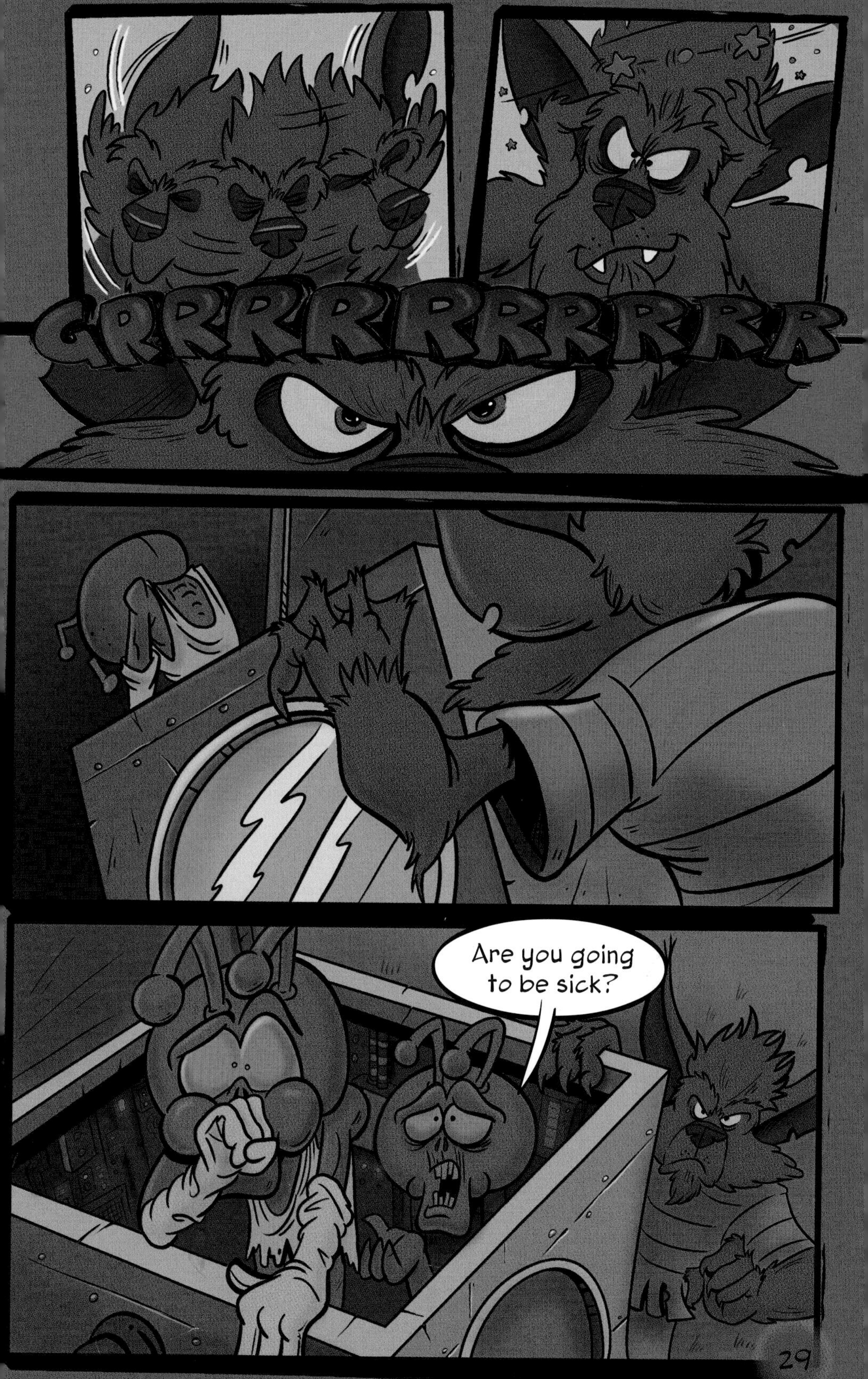
GRRRRRRRRRRR
Are you going to be sick?

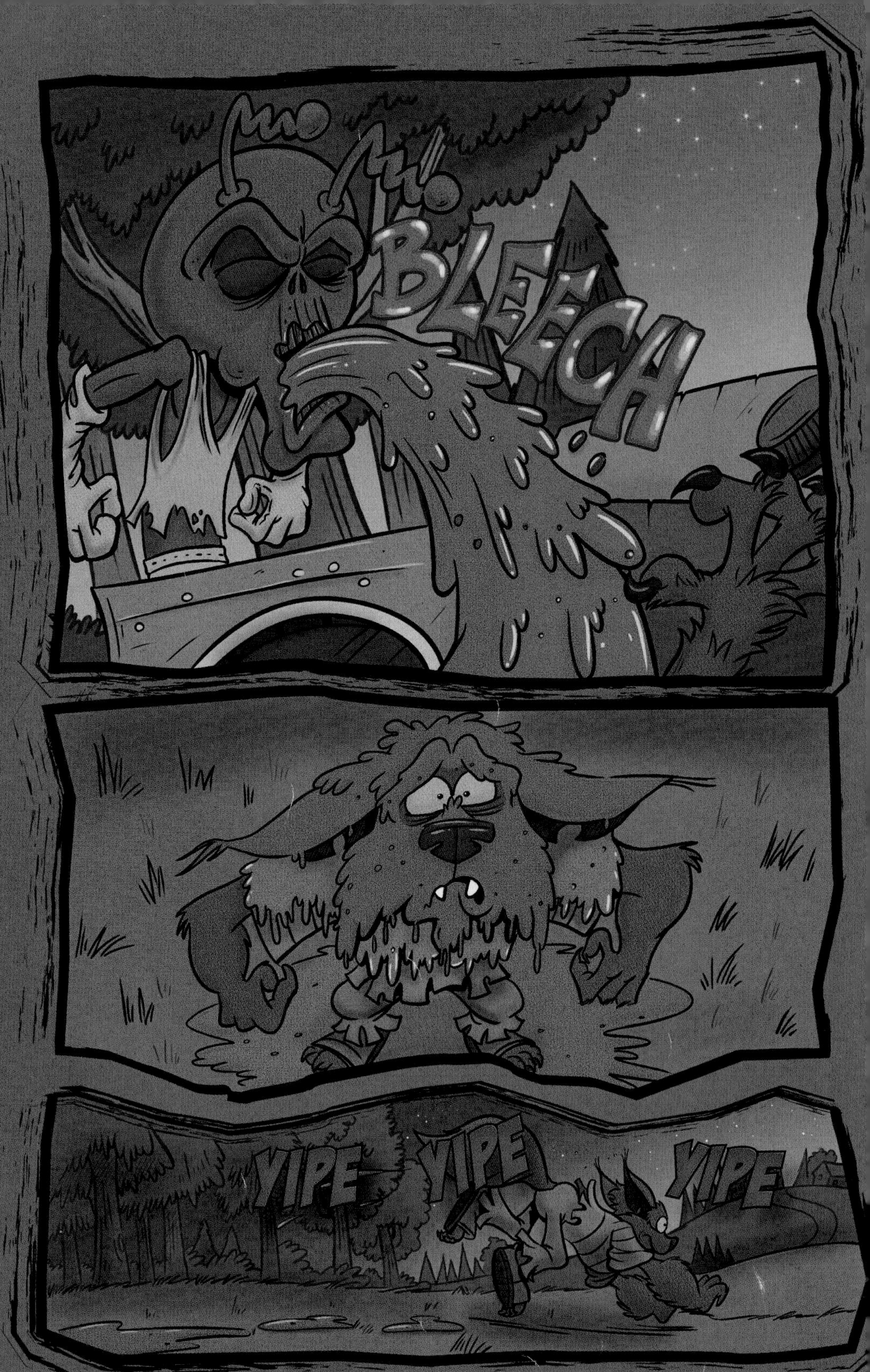
BLEECH
YIPE
YIPE
YIPE

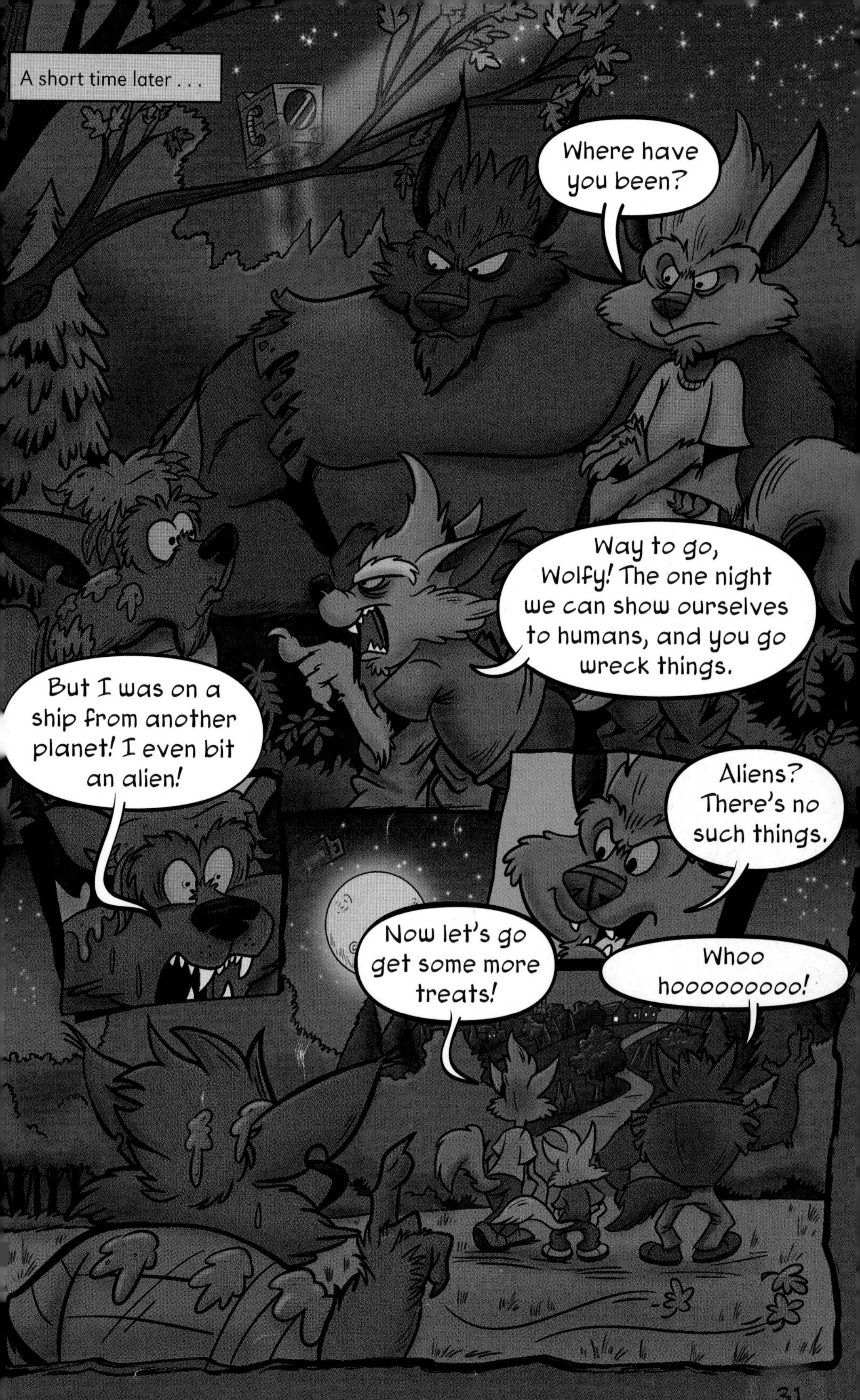
A short time later . . .
Where have you been?
Way to go, Wolfy! The one night we can show ourselves to humans, and you go wreck things.
But I was on a ship from another planet! I even bit an alien!
Aliens? There's no such things.
Now let's go get some more treats!
Whoo hoooooooooo!

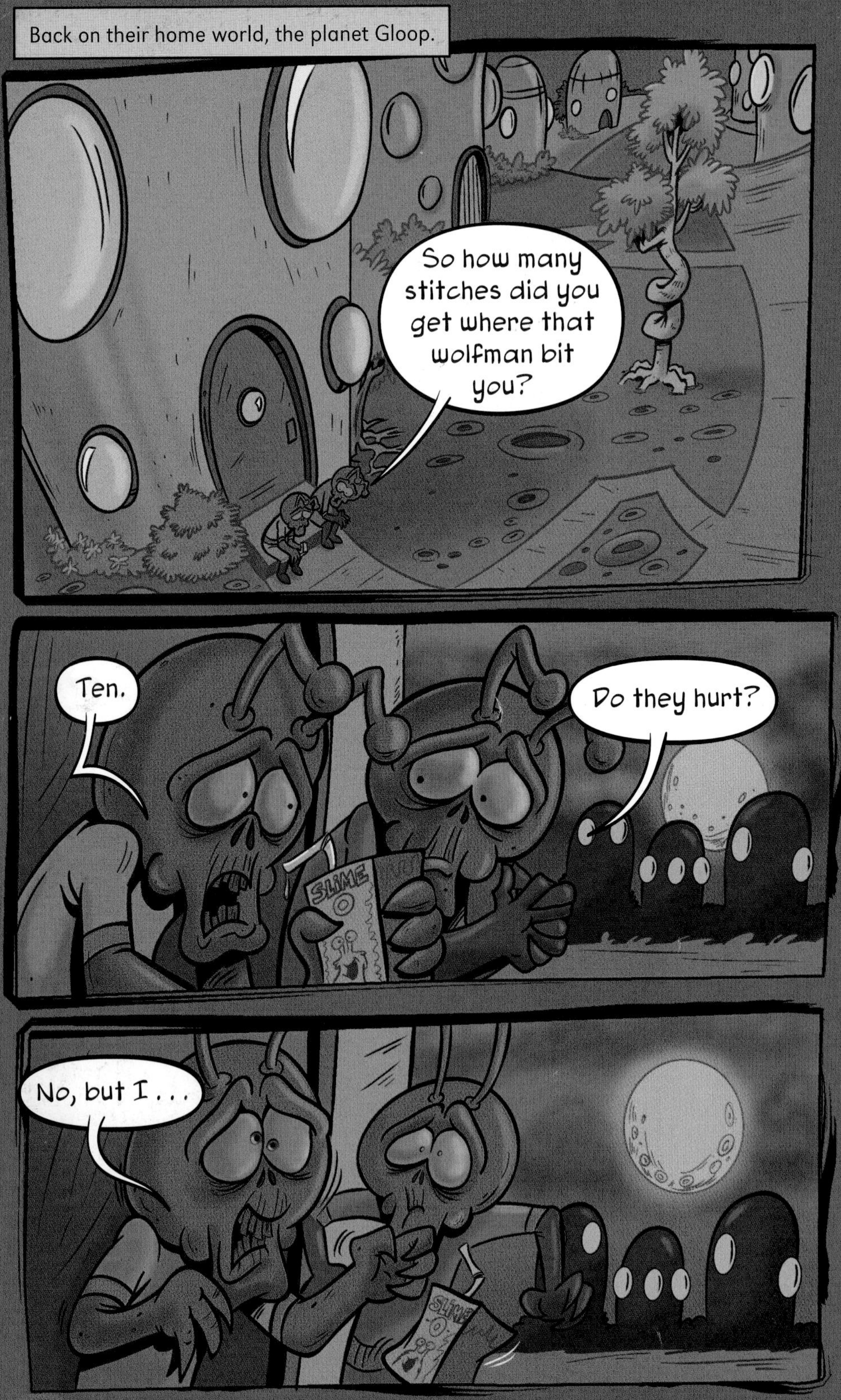
Back on their home world, the planet Gloop.
So how many stitches did you get where that wolfman bit you?
Ten.
Do they hurt?
SLIME
No, but I . . .
SLIME

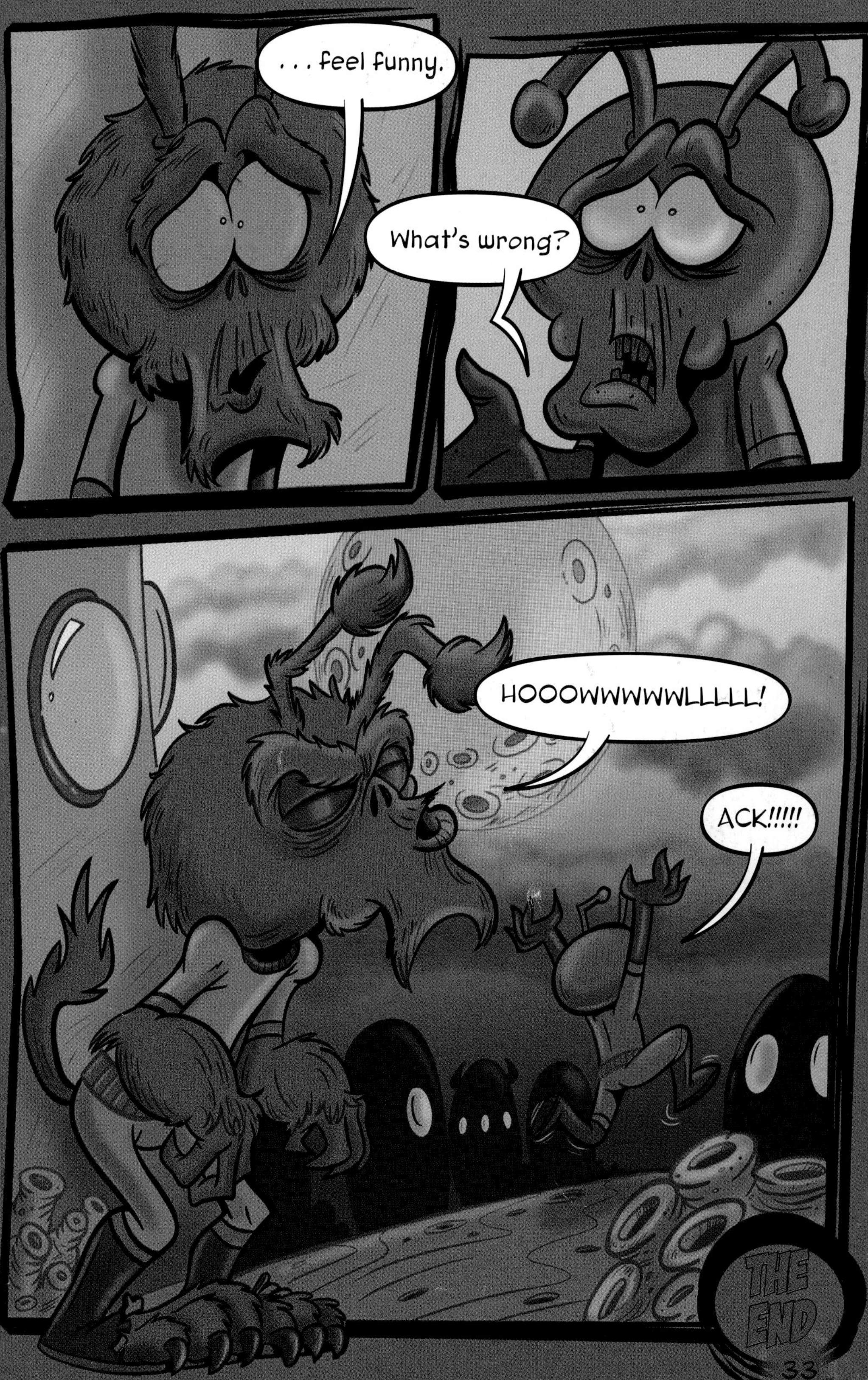
. . . feel funny.
What's wrong?
HOOOWWWWWLLLLLL!
ACK!!!!!
THE END

ABOUT THE AUTHOR

Blake A. Hoena once spent a whole weekend just watching his favorite science-fiction movies. Those movies made him wonder what kind of aliens, with their death rays and hyper-drives, couldn't actually conquer Earth. That's when he created Eek and Ack, who play at conquering Earth like earthling kids play at stopping bad guys. Blake has written more than 20 books for children, and currently lives in Minneapolis, Minnesota.

ABOUT THE ILLUSTRATOR

Steve Harpster has loved to draw funny cartoons, mean monsters, and goofy gadgets since he was able to pick up a pencil. In first grade, he avoided writing assignments by working on the pictures for stories instead. Steve was able to land a job drawing funny pictures for books, and that's really what he's best at. Steve lives in Columbus, Ohio, with his wonderful wife, Karen, and their sheepdog, Doodle.

GLOSSARY

aliens (AY-lee-uhnz)—beings from other planets

conquer (KONG-kur)—to defeat and take control of an enemy

costumes (KOSS-toomz)—clothing or outfits used to hide someone's identity

creature (KREE-chur)—a living being that is human or animal

emergency (i-MUR-juhn-see)—a sudden and dangerous situation that must be addressed quickly

harmless (HARM-liss)—not able to cause injury or damage

meteor (MEE-tee-ur)—rock or metal from space that shoots through the sky

orbiting (OR-bit-ing)—traveling around something in an elliptical pattern

sinister (SIN-uh-stur)—evil or threatening

stitches (STICH-iz)—thread or staples used to sew something back together

traditional (tra-DISH-uhn-uhl)—customs or ideas that are regularly repeated at certain times

MORE ABOUT WEREWOLVES

Wolves have been a part of children's stories for hundreds of years. "Little Red Riding Hood," "Peter and the Wolf," and "The Wolf and the Seven Young Kids" are just a few examples. But no matter what the story, the wolf is always the bad guy.

The best protection against a werewolf is pure silver. Silver bullets, daggers, and other weapons made of silver are the best defense.

In 1941, the film *The Wolf Man* made the werewolf a popular icon. The Wolf Man, Frankenstein, and Dracula are the most famous horror icons of modern times.

There are many ideas of how a person becomes a werewolf. The most popular belief is that a person must be bitten or scratched by a werewolf.

A full moon is a dangerous event for a werewolf. A human will transform into a wolf under a full moon.

The origin of the werewolf story is unknown. However, the legend is usually connected to European countries.

Many legends list the following as signs of a werewolf: eyebrows that touch, hairy palms, sharp and pointy teeth, and a middle finger that is longer than the pointer finger.

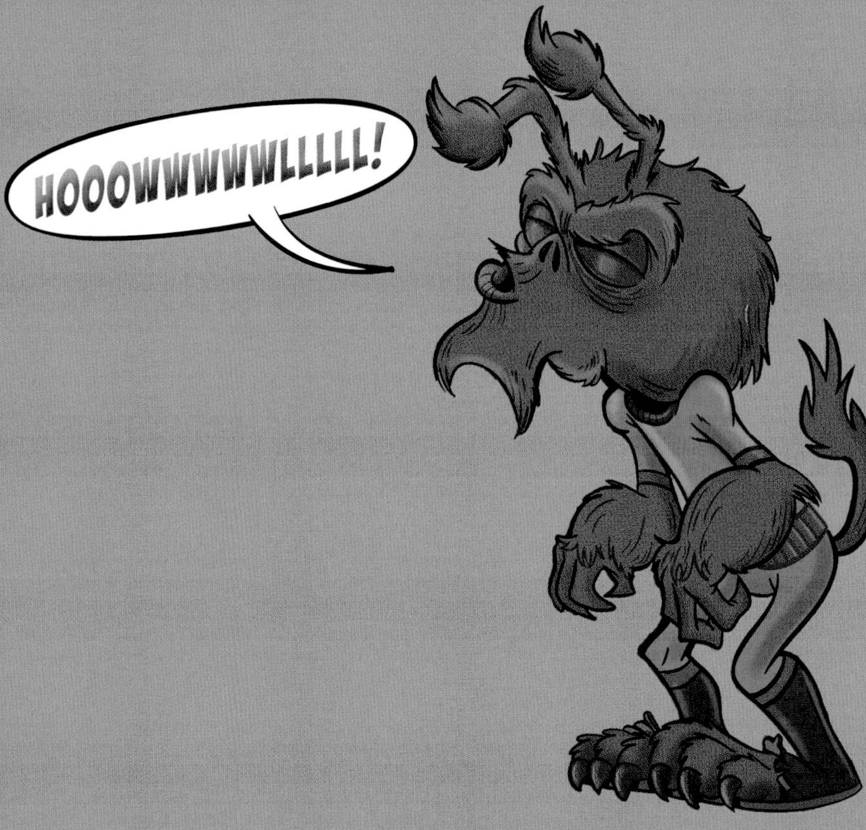
HOOOWWWWWLLLLL!

DISCUSSION QUESTIONS

1. Eek and Ack land on Earth just in time for Halloween. If you were to introduce a holiday to aliens, which holiday would you pick and why?

2. If you were an alien, what would your alien name be? Why?

3. If you had to pick, would you rather be an alien or a werewolf? Why?

WRITING PROMPTS

1. Eek and Ack wear a ballerina dress and a cape to blend in with earthlings. If you were an alien, what would you wear to blend in? Write a paragraph describing your disguise and draw a picture.

2. Eek and Ack try to sneak onto Earth during a meteor storm. If you were an alien, how would you get to Earth? Write a detailed plan.

3. Eek and Ack live on the planet Gloop. Make up a new planet and write a paragraph about it. Be sure to name it and describe what it looks like.

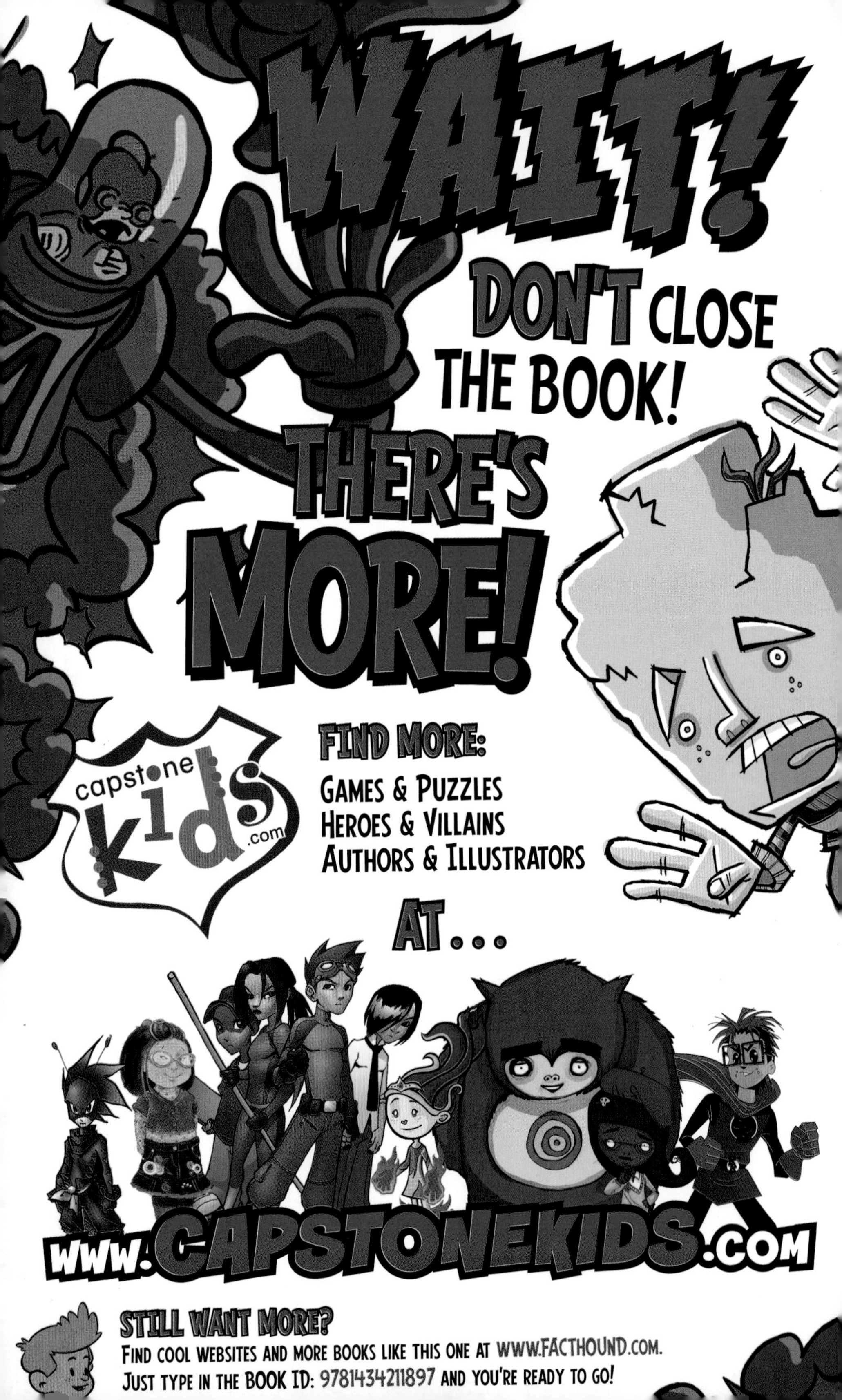

WAIT!
DON'T CLOSE THE BOOK!
THERE'S MORE!
capstone kids .com
FIND MORE:
GAMES & PUZZLES
HEROES & VILLAINS
AUTHORS & ILLUSTRATORS
AT...
WWW.CAPSTONEKIDS.COM
STILL WANT MORE?
FIND COOL WEBSITES AND MORE BOOKS LIKE THIS ONE AT WWW.FACTHOUND.COM.
JUST TYPE IN THE BOOK ID: 9781434211897 AND YOU'RE READY TO GO!

5/1/15